LOVE ODYSSEY

ROBERTA SERET

WAYZGOOSE PRESS

Editing by Maggie Sokolik

Cover design by D.J. Rogers, Book Branders

ISBN: 978-1938757884

This is a work of fiction.

- There was no doctor who worked within Ceausescu's government to begin the revolution or to overthrow the dictator.
- The love story and characters do not represent anyone in history or in the present.

72721

"Three thousand years have not changed the human condition in this respect: we are still lovers and victims of the will to violence, and so long as we are, Homer will be read as its truest interpretation."

— FROM THE INTRODUCTION BY BERNARD KNOW TO HOMER'S *THE ILIAD* (ROBERT FAGLES, TRANSLATOR)

IN APPRECIATION

No book is written alone.

Words and thoughts come alive on the page only after they are shared with those the author respects. I have been fortunate to have family and friends who have believed in me. For without them, my literary world could not have taken shape.

My deepest appreciation goes to each one of you:

Maggie Sokolik, Senior Fiction Editor of Wayzgoose Press; Dorothy Zemach, publisher of Wayzgoose Press; DJ Rogers, Book Branders, for her artistic book jacket, Linda Langton, my literary agent; Marcia Rockwood, my editor; Mridula Agarwal, my right hand and tech Guru; Natalia Donofrio, my web designer; Greenwich Pen Women: Anita Keire, Ginger Heller, Deb Weir, and Kyle Ridley.

My friends of many years: Judith Vogel, Leslie and Norman Leben, Lydia Eviatar, Judith Auslander, Raffaella Depero, Nancy Cushing-Jones, Will Nix, Elise Strauss, Nina Saglimbeni, Candida Iodice, Andreea Mihut, Ioana and Eugen Mihut, and Sandra Segal.

My sons: Greg and Cliff; my daughters-in-law: Hally and Arielle: my grandchildren: Annabel, Sam, Jack.

And my husband, Michel, who always at my side, has shared his story and our journey. Without his *joie de vivre* and optimism, these books would not have come to be.

Thank you all,
Roberta

To Greg, Cliff, Hally, Arielle, Annabel, Sam, Jack

My greatest wish has been to give you all I have learned.

My Odyssey—with Love—is for you.

INTRODUCTION

Dear Reader,

I invite you to go on a voyage with me to Transylvania where my imagination has borrowed political intrigues to create a different view of Literature. Facts fuse with fiction in *Transylvanian Trilogy.*

Gift of Diamonds, Love Odyssey, and *Treasure Seekers*—each book of the trilogy can be read independently or interchanged, depending on the reader's choice. The main characters are Mica, Anca, Cristina, and Marina, four friends since their teenaged days in Transylvania, who appear and reappear in each book. They were known in their little town as best friends, the Four Musketeers, *Poets of their Lives.*

Gift of Diamonds is Mica's story and her escape with rare colored diamonds as Communism in Romania explodes under dictator, Ceausescu.

Love Odyssey is Anca's quest as she escapes alone while pregnant from those who have targeted her.

Marina and Cristina take center stage in *Treasure Seekers* when they are successful women living in New York City and Paris, and vacation together to exotic Turkey to fall, unexpectedly, into a web of terrorists.

The stories flow together amidst Romania's politics. I have used the historical settings as a novelist would—to enhance the fictional storyline. Yet, I must confess, I have sometimes been tempted to make the history a little more exciting with touches of imagination. Accordingly, I've taken liberties under the guise of "poetic license" with time and place to recreate a literary fresco of Romania's second half of the 20th century. The history is the "back-drop curtain" of the novels, not center stage.

I have used Romania's dictatorial regimes to create an atmosphere of deceit that poisoned all Romanians during the Fascist and Communist years. One form of totalitarian government led to another. These were times of secret police, informers, fear, lies, double-crossing, dehumanization, shredding of documents, the destruction of the human soul. What we know today about these times is still masked with inconsistencies and ambiguities to cover up the Truth.

Yet the world I offer you is of Fiction, and I use four female characters as dramatic voices. Each woman of the trilogy takes center stage to create her own life as she journeys through political events to survive. Each one becomes involved with history and forges forward in an existentialist need to direct her own destiny. Sometimes, the four friends find challenges that are stronger than their willpower. Those are the times when the fictional protagonists merge and interact with factual events. It is then that their courage evokes exciting narratives. Fiction that could not exist without Truth.

I hope you enjoy this colorful kaleidoscope of Fact with Fiction, Truth with Crimes, History and Art, Strife with Love. For it is from my heart that I offer you these stories from Transylvania.

Roberta Seret, Ph.D.

PROLOGUE

I HAVE OFTEN TRIED to understand love.

Is there a logic, a pattern, a process? Does it begin as a chemical reaction? Does the heart tell reason that there is no place for logic? Or does the mind direct all feelings? How does it happen that love can transport us to a state of being that we have never known before? And why do we journey so far, so blindly, so willingly, for the person we love?

I have wondered if we love only once. Or can we love different people with different loves at different times? Is it possible that love can transform itself into something sinister and unrecognizable and still be love? And if we should choose to reject love completely, what is life without loving?

My story is one of love, colored with tender moments of pleasure and heights of ecstasy. But it is also shadowed gray when love was crushed by shame, when lies turned passion to pain.

On an autumn night in Transylvania, October 1970, the golden days of yellow leaves had turned into smoky evenings tinged with the smell of wood-burning fireplaces. Communism was at its peak under Nicolae Ceausescu. No one could do what they wanted unless the government approved. I was outspoken, independent, and uncooperative. I was being watched.

Alec, my best friend from childhood, had come to our two-room cottage late at night to give me and Petre, my husband of three years, some confidential information. I remember the storm that night, with its lightning and thunder, and even hail. But luck was in our favor; the police preferred to stay indoors, drinking with their buddies rather than patrolling the town or watching people like us.

Alec had been my father's student at the Technical University of Civil Engineering and his helper on Sundays in our basement, where they both sent secret messages to people in other countries. He had graduated to become the chief engineer at the Ministry of Agriculture. Petre was a doctor, specializing in endocrinology. He was in charge of the clinic in our small town, Dova.

Alec came to tell us he had news: one of the Austrian tractors the government was using to work the farms was defective. The parts weren't available in Romania and the tractor would have to be sent to Vienna for repairs. Alec knew that I was pregnant. He had been working on a plan to get me out of Romania, to hide me in the tractor as it traveled from Transylvania to Budapest and then by hydrofoil up the Danube to trustworthy contacts in Vienna.

"I won't go," I told Alec and Petre.

Petre insisted. "Anca, this is your only chance. You can't have a baby in this country."

"I will not leave without you."

"I'll follow," he promised.

Alec persisted. "I can make another defective tractor for Petre in two months by detaching some wires needed to start the motor," he told me. "Your husband can leave then. But you must take this one first."

Petre paced our small living room. I had never seen him so

agitated before. He was almost shouting at me. "The secret police have started an investigation on you. I know this from a patient. Someone I trust."

"How will I be transported to Budapest?" I asked them. "The borders are locked as tight as an iron gate."

"The tractor will be hauled in a truck from our town to Budapest," Alec answered. "I'll create space for you under the tractor's seat where you'll be hidden."

"What about food and water?"

"It'll be next to where you'll lay comfortably on a mattress."

"Comfortably?" I said, raising my voice. "Do you realize what will happen to me if the secret police come searching with their dogs?"

Alec shook his head. "As director of the agricultural project, I have the right to escort the tractor from here to Budapest and onto the hydrofoil, which I will do. Once on the hydrofoil, you'll be on the Danube and safe."

Petre took my hand. "Alec will protect you. He has the contacts from the Danube to the hotel in Vienna, and then…"

"No! It's too risky."

"You must take this opportunity," Petre insisted. "The chief of the region is in charge of your case. He has proof you've given antibiotics to Gypsies[1] and noncommunists. The police will very likely torture you. You could lose the baby."

I was crying, pleading my case to both men, but as I felt the baby kick inside me, I knew they were right. "Petre, you promise to take the next available tractor?"

"Yes," he assured me. "I'll be at your side when you give birth. You have my word."

Was I wrong to have agreed? I can't help but wonder now: what was Petre's true motive for getting me out of the country? Did he know then that his promise to follow me in just two months was simply a subterfuge? Over the years, I have tried to analyze the truth as well as the lies. I've wanted to forgive Petre, to feel less for him, to live my life guided by reason—and accept my fate. I have struggled with this. Then one morning, a newspaper and a telephone call tore my ordered world apart.

---

1. I use the term *Gypsy* with no intention of disrespect. The official term is *Roma,* but I use *Gypsy* as a colloquial word, spoken by Europeans in their daily conversations.

PART I

PENELOPE AND ODYSSEUS

SUNDAY, DECEMBER 10, 1989

Penelope with Odysseus's armor—Francis Legatt Chantrey (1781–1841)

1

NEW YORK CITY

> *So that I could meet the Odysseus I long for. Yet the evil is endurable, when one cries through the days, with heart constantly troubled.*
>
> — HOMER, *THE ODYSSEY*, BOOK 20

RUBBING SLEEP FROM HER EYES, Anca opened the front door of her Upper East Side apartment and picked up the Sunday *New York Times.* The kitchen was shadowed in morning darkness as she placed the newspaper on the marble counter and mechanically opened the refrigerator to take out a can of espresso beans.

She stared at her face reflected on the metal container as if she were a stranger, observing the straight black hair cropped short, hazel-green eyes so sleepy that the almond slits seemed buried within high cheekbones. The lips looked full above the pointed chin, and the oval face appeared younger than its forty-two years. She stretched her body in her blue bathrobe and tried to get her thin, five-foot-seven shape to fill the face of the silver container by tilting it this way and that.

While the coffee was brewing, she scanned the first page of the *Times*. She was stopped cold by one particular headline: *Romania and Iran: Partners in Gold and Evil.*

"Twenty years of friendship and billions of dollars in trade between Romania and Iran," the article read. "First with Shah Reza Pahlavi, then with Ayatollah Khomeini, and now with Iran's new president, Rafsanjani, with whom Ceausescu has a *personal, financial relationship.* The question is what are they planning together? Authorities talk about gold. An investigation has been traced to Transylvania in Romania."

Anca took a deep breath. Transylvania. At this moment it was tied to a gold scandal. But, she also remembered her country as the place where her loving had its beginning and she could still feel his touch, his lips caressing her body. Such deep pleasure, wanting more and more.

"Would you like a glass of wine?"

It was during the harvest, a September evening when pine trees in Romania turned gold and the Gypsies gathered grapes.

Anca closed her eyes to keep the memory alive. She could feel Petre's presence, strong and soft.

"The wine from the barrel is warm."

The fiddler played a Gypsy song, "Te iubesc pe vesnicie"—I will love you forever.

Was she strong enough for feelings she had never experienced before?

She allowed the wine to cloud her mind and followed for the first time as he led her along a path, through the valley. He caressed her cheeks and she closed her eyes, the wine making her bold. He brought her closer, held her tighter, and laid her lovingly in a bed of golden leaves.

The next morning, with the memory of lovemaking inside her, she went to the Gypsy camp in their small town and overheard a

Gypsy saying, "A woman loves only one man in her life." Anca wondered, *Was that a prophecy for me?*

She recalled how each year the wine harvest varied by a few days depending on nature's whims and summer rains. In Romania, there was no calendar to tell the farmers when to start picking the grapes. Instead, they knew because of the Gypsies who wandered in from Hungary and Serbia. They arrived saying that they had come to work; the grapes were ready. Then, on the last day of the harvest, they disappeared, late at night, not to be seen until the next year when the grapes had ripened again.

───────

Anca wiped tears from her cheek remembering how three years later, Petre had sealed her fate with plans for her escape. To his mission he had remained true—working to free Romania from a dictator, while Anca had been sent to New York, alone.

2

BUCHAREST, ROMANIA

> *Sing in me, muse, and through me tell the story of that man skilled in all ways of contending, the wanderer, harried for years on end.*

— HOMER, *THE ODYSSEY*, BOOK 1

"*ATENTIE*. STOP. DON'T MOVE."

"Oh, it's you, Petre. Sorry," a Romanian guard said as he put the pistol back inside his coat. "I didn't recognize you in that long coat." He bowed to the tall blond man who had barely flinched at the sight of the gun.

"I'm visiting the Leader," Petre answered, pointing to his black doctor's bag and taking off his wool hat and scarf. He walked through the concrete tunnel that led to Ceausescu's underground bunker system. The hidden labyrinth, located beneath the presidential palace, was stocked with food, medicine and supplies for the Ceausescu family and their secret police force. In case of an uprising, the dictator could live here for several months. The complex also included offices, prison cells, a clinic, a cinema, and a dozen bedrooms. There was even an enclosed garage with a car from which Ceausescu and his family could flee, should they need to.

Petre passed through the archway that connected the medical dispensary to Ceausescu's private quarters.

"It would have been easier for me to examine him in my office," Petre thought, as he passed his medical suite. He climbed up a set of steps that led to an opulent room that was shining bright beneath several Baccarat crystal chandeliers. *So odd*, Petre thought. *Baccarat in an underground bunker.*

When he knocked on the door, a butler answered, *"Da?"* and Petre turned the crystal doorknob. Each time he turned the door-knob, he thought of Gheorgheiu-Dej, Romania's dictator before Ceausescu, a man who had met his end when the doorknob to his bathroom had been secretly filled with radioactive matter. He had died of cancer.

"Wash your hands first," the butler said to Petre, handing him a bowl of water and a towel. They both knew the routine Ceausescu requested of each guest. He didn't trust anyone, wouldn't shake hands, and was always suspicious of poison hidden somewhere on their person.

The dictator walked into the room, and without greeting Petre, stated, "I'm not well."

"Sorry, sir. I will see what the problem is."

"I know what the problem is!" Ceausescu yelled. "I've had a headache all night and couldn't sleep. Went to the bathroom every hour. Too much beer last night."

"Sir, maybe your blood pressure is high, or your diabetes is unregulated. I can test your sugar level."

"Just tell me if I'm strong enough to travel."

Petre didn't answer for fear of angering the dictator further. Instead, he took a blood pressure gauge from his black bag.

"Don't you have anything more modern than that?" Ceausescu

snapped at him. "Why do you think I let you leave this country to go to meetings? The Germans or Austrians must have something more elaborate than that ridiculous blood snake."

Petre tried to smile at what he pretended was a joke. He realized Ceausescu was nervous. Perhaps he knows an uprising is brewing? *I'll have to ask my men and find out if there's been a leak.* Or perhaps Ceausescu could see the writing on the wall and that was why he was going to Tehran. Safer banking privacy than in Switzerland. He had to put his fortune somewhere.

"President, sir, this is all that is available to measure blood pressure." Petre put his stethoscope under the dictator's pajamas and bathrobe to listen to his breathing. *Yes, he's nervous,* Petre thought as he moved the stethoscope on Ceausescu's back and concentrated on the rapid breathing and wheezing. *He's probably wondering if Rafsanjani will receive him with a parade and red carpet. Certainly, the Iranian president will secretly accept his fortune.*

"Petre!" Ceausescu yelled, breaking him from his musing. "What's taking you so long? I asked you a question. Should I increase the dosage of my insulin?"

"Do you have symptoms, sir?"

"What does that mean?"

"Do you have an increased need to urinate? Increase in thirst? Increased appetite?"

"Of course. It's all the fault of the beer I drank last night. I was feeling uncomfortable. General Babescu has been plotting against me."

Petre listened intently, but maintained a bland façade.

"With the Russians. With Gorbachev. I invited him here last night for dinner with his wife and daughter. Afterwards, they had to be detained and interrogated. I couldn't let them return home."

Petre had known General Babescu well. He was the minister of defense and worked with Ian Ileyesco, Ceausescu's right-hand man.

As Petre asked Ceausescu to turn around and placed the stethoscope next to his heart, he tried to figure out who had ratted out the general.

A guard entered the room. "Sir." He addressed the dictator with his head bent low. "Excuse me, sir, for interrupting... your wife said I should tell you that your son, Nicu-..."

"What's the matter with him *now?*"

"I don't know, sir, but your wife said to come right away."

"That's enough, Petre. You're not helping me anyway. Leave me some medicine for my blood pressure and headaches. Check the insulin dosage."

"Yes, sir, of course."

Ceausescu left, slamming the door.

Petre quietly departed and reemerged in the clinic. A guard approached him, bowed deferentially, and saluted to him before speaking.

"Are you expecting any patients that I should bring to you?"

Petre shrugged. "Maybe," he answered.

The guard whispered to another guard. "Must be someone important if the person is to be seen by Ceausescu's private doctor. Probably a terrorist Ceausescu has taken as his personal guard."

Petre pretended he hadn't heard their hushed chatter. Instead, he thought angrily of the terrorists infiltrating his country. Petre had learned from his contacts that Ceausescu's business partners–Gaddafi and Arafat–were supplying him with personal, protective *soldiers.*

"What do we Romanians have to do with all these people? They're trouble," a guard complained. "We're Christians."

The guards stopped talking abruptly and looked around, afraid that someone might have heard them. If that should happen, they'd be denounced. One of them moved closer to Petre and said, "Uranium and plutonium. Centrifuges. Atomic reactors. Terrorists. I wish they'd get out of our country before we're blamed by the entire world for starting a nuclear war."

Petre shrugged again. "What do I know about politics?" he replied, trying to appear calm while controlling his anger and defiance.

Petre passed through the archway that connected the medical dispensary to the prison. Another guard saluted him and Petre waved him away so he could be alone in the clinic. When the door closed behind him, he took two keys from his pocket. He opened a metal cabinet and took out five vials of penicillin from a medicine chest, and then put them in his bag and locked the chest and cabinet. He returned the keys to his coat pocket and left.

He moved toward a narrow opening in the tunnel that was hidden behind a stone pillar. While the guards were busy talking, he removed two loose bricks from the wall. In a quick moment, he took several vials of tetracycline and put the antibiotics in his pocket. As he returned the bricks, he eyed a rat scurrying from its hiding place.

Hearing a clanging of chains, he turned his attention down the hallway to a guard who was leading a bound man through the dark tunnel. The man was bleeding, and the guard continued to interrogate him relentlessly.

Petre came out of his hiding place and pretended he hadn't seen the guard with his terrified victim. He didn't want to make a scene, despite his desire to try and stop the guard's cruelty.

To all eyes in the dark tunnel, Ceausescu's personal doctor was simply doing his duty. Putting medicines in his bag was part of his work. The doctor's importance gave the guards little reason to doubt him at all.

Petre climbed up a small staircase that led to a trap door and exited. He didn't want anyone to see him. He pushed open the heavy lid and walked into an outdoor garden filled with dry brush.

Picking up a handful of leaves, he covered the trap door and sealed Hades from the rest of the world.

3

NEW YORK CITY

A<small>NCA HEARD</small> the coffee splash inside the coffeepot. She went to the
stove, poured herself a cup, and returned to the *Times*.

> Intelligence officials have located a private bank in Tehran
> where Ceausescu has been depositing his fortune, which
> includes tons of gold bullion bars and gold coins from
> payments he received in exchange for allowing Romanian
> Jews and ethnic Germans to leave the country for Canada,
> the United States, Israel, and Germany. The money trail has
> led investigators to a nuclear facility hidden in Transylva-
> nia, built by Ceausescu for his partners Muammar Gaddafi
> of Libya, Ayatollah Rafsanjani of Iran, Yassir Arafat of the
> PLO, Kim Il-Sung of North Korea, and Saddam Hussein of
> Iraq.

On the bottom of the page were photos of the leaders.

Ceausescu had amassed a fortune. His goal was to be the
richest man in Eastern Europe, Anca thought while studying the

photos. *Some communist,* she thought. These photos of Ceausescu smiling with the world's corrupt leaders meant trouble.

The telephone rang, and Anca picked it up on the second ring. "Hello?"

No one answered.

"Hello?" she said again. She thought it might be Mica, her childhood friend, reconfirming the time they would meet that afternoon. But, whoever was on the other end wasn't responding. She hung up and continued reading. The telephone rang again.

"Hello?" she said, now hoping it might be her daughter, Sandra, calling from college. However, that made little sense since they had just spoken the previous night.

Anca heard a muffled sound and then a click. She looked around the kitchen, wondering if she should be alarmed. She studied the ceiling and walls–maybe her apartment had been bugged.

Her thoughts immediately went to the day before. Every Saturday for the past two years, Anca had met with a group of colleagues who'd lived in Eastern Europe at the New York Voice of America radio station. They discussed the important news of the week, and then each one would transmit a secret message over the radio to the people living in their native countries. At three o'clock, Anca had broadcast her message:

In this Christmas season, Romanians should work together to build up their country and not allow their leader to sacrifice them for his terrorist goals.

Anca suspected that her silent telephone callers might be Romania's secret police, the Securitate. When she arrived home after the broadcast, there was an unsigned, typed note in her mailbox:

REMEMBER YOU ARE A MOTHER.

She quickly called Sandra to make sure her daughter was safe. Sandra chatted with her for several minutes and then said she was okay, but had to go.

Anca was shaken by the message and considered showing it to her director at Voice of America. Finally, she changed her mind. She didn't want an investigation, and she didn't want someone to contact Sandra. Instead, she ripped up the note and kept the threat secret.

She had understood the message. Anca had lived the first half of her life in Romania, and she knew well the workings of the secret police. It wasn't the first time they had harassed her. She remembered her days as a doctor in Transylvania. Why was she being threatened now, after so many years, and in New York? It couldn't be a coincidence, she realized. She was well aware that no Romanian, not even a Romanian émigré living in the States, could criticize Ceausescu without consequences.

The telephone rang again. Anca let it ring, and then changed her mind and picked it up once more.

"Hello!" she yelled. "Who is this? What do you want?"

All she could hear was a distant voice mumbling in a foreign language—blurred sounds, and then a click again.

Anca thought that she might have been too bold on the radio. She feared that the Romanian secret police would never leave her alone until they stopped her from speaking. They had an old vendetta against her from her youth. Or was something else happening—something new?

She stared at the telephone, wondering what to do, as images of the past returned.

The first time she had seen Petre was the summer of 1965, several months before Ceausescu had come into power. The anti-communists were orga-nizing an uprising in Transylvania to try to stop the new dictator from taking power. Anca had been at the library in Cluj studying, but at the sound of a crowd cheering, she ran to the window.

A young man holding a bullhorn stood on a platform. He looked foreign—so tall and blond—but he spoke Romanian.

She was drawn to him. Curious, she left the library to join the crowd.

"Prieteni, friends, listen to me," she heard the young man shout. "Haven't you had enough of communism? Let's all unite and finish this evil!"

There were chants, hoorays, and applause from the crowd.

"Move on! Move on!" the police roared, closing in.

"Go home!" the soldiers warned.

The crowd threw rocks. Students set fire to the town hall and the police sprayed them with water hoses. Anca ran away. Frightened, she hid behind some trees. Nearby, sitting against a building, was the same young man who had spoken. Anca felt a gnawing pull towards him. He was different—intense and driven. She felt his torment. She thought about helping him, but then a wagon stopped in front of him and he was gone.

She tried to refocus on the present. She touched the walls of her kitchen and repeated the mantra she spoke in times of stress. "I'm safe. I'm in America. I practice medicine at New York Hospital."

She closed her eyes so as to block the young man's haunting stare from her mind. His memory still lived on, even nineteen years after she had escaped from Romania in 1970.

In 1965, when Ceausescu took power, Anca was already a doctor, specializing in infectious diseases, but since she had never joined the Communist Youth Party she couldn't work in a major city like Cluj. She had to take a job that the government offered her in Dova, a remote town in Transylvania. Not many doctors would have chosen to work there, where three thousand peasants were suffering from a typhus epidemic.

In those days, in that part of Transylvania, there was no electricity, no medicine, no antibiotics, no sterilization—only homemade *tuica*—a plum brandy that the peasants made themselves. They used it as an anesthetic or drank instead of water.

Despite the hardships, it was an exciting time of her life, a time of new beginnings. It was in Dova that Anca had unexpectedly crossed paths with the same young man with the intense eyes. His name was Petre, and he was the chief physician of the clinic where she was working. They fell in love, married, and lived together for three years. In spite of their difficult work fighting typhus and caring for patients, it had been a special time when she discovered love.

She couldn't stop thinking about it this morning, and she had to ask herself, *Why this morning in particular?* Perhaps because she was so occupied in analyzing her message on the Voice of America broadcast from the day before and the threatening note, or the morning's *Times* article, the photos, and the suspicious phone calls. All these things were pulling her back to her past life in Transylvania.

"Anca," Petre called from the small consultation room. "I'll meet you here at the dispensary when you finish your rounds. I'm waiting for a delivery. I don't want anyone to know it's the typhus vaccines."

"Fine, I'm taking Dory to help me. I hope to be back for lunch." She handed her twelve-year-old helper a box of supplies. Dory's dream was to be a doctor.

"Did you vaccinate yourself?" Petre asked.

"Yes, yesterday. Dory, too. No side effects." She touched the boy's forehead to make sure he wasn't warm.

Anca went to a small hidden alcove where there was a refrigerator. She looked around to make sure she was alone. She knew the medicines were very valuable, and non-existent in Transylvania. To have them was equal to having a secret treasure. They saved lives, but no one in a position of authority was to know.

She opened the refrigerator's lock and took out the vaccines and several vials of tetracycline and hid them in a compartment at the bottom of her black bag. She put on a pair of plastic gloves and walked out of the alcove to find Dory. She gave him a pair of gloves as well.

"You carry the machine and the spray hose for the DDT," she instructed the boy. "We'll visit several houses this morning."

"Okay, Dr. Rodescu. Do you want me to carry your bag?"

"No, I'll take it." She couldn't trust anyone with the medicines, not even Dory.

As Anca and Dory walked down the staircase, she felt something soft under her foot—a dead rat. She pushed it to the side without a word so as not to alarm the boy. They walked through the muddy streets of the village and hardly spoke.

She approached a cottage in Gypsy town and knocked on the half-opened door. She and Dory entered. The one-room house was poorly lit and smelled bad.

The leader of the Gypsies, Evdochia, greeted her. It was the first time that Anca had met her, although she had seen her before from a distance.

"Dr. Rodescu," the Gypsy begged her, "please help my baby boy."

Anca walked over to the small bed where the child lay wheezing. His eyelids were swollen and pink cuts and scabs covered his lips.

"He's on fire," his mother cried. The boy's wheezing became fainter.

Anca examined the one-year-old's frail chest and gazed at the oozing blotches on his skin. She tried to appear calm as she took the child's temperature. "I have something special for you," she said, as she took an orange out of her bag and gave it to the little boy.

He looked at her with his dark feverish eyes and took the fruit.

Evdochia said, "It looks like the sun." Then the Gypsy looked down and cried. "Don't take him to the hospital. He'll never come back if he goes there."

Anca knelt on the floor next to the boy and listened to his chest with her stethoscope. His gasping breath was weak.

"Best for him not to leave you," Anca told the mother. "I have a special medicine for him and for you. I have food, too."

Dory gave the Gypsy fruit, cheese, and bread while Anca took the vaccines and antibiotics from her bag. Evdochia fell on her knees and tried to kiss Anca's shoes, but Anca took her hand and pulled her up. She said to Dory, "Spray DDT on everything, on all the furniture, the floors, the walls, even the clothes. Everything is contagious."

She turned to Evdochia. "Can you show Dory where your clothes are? He'll boil them. Your cow has to be quarantined in the barn. Don't drink her milk. Let me vaccinate you now and I'll be back tomorrow." Anca also vaccinated the child. "I'll bring you and your son something sweet to eat," she told the Gypsy.

4

BUCHAREST, ROMANIA

> The movements which work revolutions in the world are born out of the dreams and visions in a peasant's heart on the hillside.
>
> — HOMER, *THE ODYSSEY*, BOOK 12

PETRE WALKED through the *Cismigiu Gardens* and looked surreptitiously for anything suspicious, such as too many police on the street, or shady-looking people who could be informers. He noticed there was no one from the secret police at the front gate. No one would ordinarily detect them, but Petre would—he knew their demeanor.

As Petre continued toward the main street, Calea Victoriei, he decided not to take the trolley to his apartment, but to go by foot. From time to time, he looked over his shoulder, never letting his guard down.

He closed the top button of his old coat and tried to block out the cold, sneezing from time to time as he wiped away the city's dust from his face and eyes. Everything looked blurry from pollution. Even the trees and bushes were covered with particles of dirt. The streets remained dismal and dark, made even blacker by abandoned buildings smeared with tar.

He passed a store and saw nearly a hundred people waiting outside. It looked like a lineup in a prison yard. They were mostly old men and women, forgotten souls dressed in layers of ragged clothes. *The same victims and same lines as twenty-four years ago when I first returned to Romania from America,* he thought sadly. In a familiar move, he hefted his doctor's bag with resignation.

Over the years, Petre had adopted a ready smile that quickly appeared on his face, even if he wasn't happy. He used it in a defensive way, usually to stop someone from asking him a question. Whenever he wanted to retreat, he would smile, thereby camouflaging his real nature.

He was an ambitious man, driven by an obsession to help his people, be it as a doctor or as a leader wanting to change the corruption and tyranny in his country. When alone, he suffered, unable to give his fellow Romanians the better life they deserved.

Despite his own life of limited happiness, Petre was still a vibrant and attractive man. At forty-six, with a full head of blond hair, he looked youthful and energetic. With his narrow, six-foot one frame, he moved like a fox, although more shy than sly. His fine feature—the aquiline nose and angular cheekbones—had a mysterious allure.

He kept his inner world to himself and closed out friends when they tried to come too near. He had never remarried after his divorce from Anca. He knew people wondered why. To prevent curiosity, he simply traded his sociability for solitude, and transformed his forthrightness to a distant reserve. He discouraged those who tried to interfere with his private life or even his thoughts. He kept his secrets locked in his heart.

Petre's goal was to start a revolution and bring down Ceausescu, to put an end to the terrorists being trained in Romania, and to destroy the regime's nuclear facility. He believed he was destined to do these things. He would not stop until he had achieved his goals.

He was a man of many facets, but he didn't want the people he worked with to realize that. He needed to cooperate with Ceausescu and his inner circle. He had to appear to be like them and to share their love of luxury and privilege, otherwise, they wouldn't trust him. Yet he didn't want to lose his true self. He was a man of ideals, ready to sacrifice everything, as he had done with his wife and daughter. Petre was a man living with two faces.

Nothing changes in Bucharest, he thought as he continued his walk through the city. There's no food, little electricity, heat, light, but Ceausescu is the richest man in Eastern Europe because of his friends in Iran, Libya, Iraq, and North Korea. They were a gang of bandits, no better than thugs, with evil schemes of ill-gotten gains.

Soon, soon, I will change things, he thought.

He stopped walking when he encountered a long line of people waiting outside a grocery store. The pale glare of the day's beginning cast a half-shadow on their faces, giving them a semblance of dead spirits. He moved to the end of the line, wanting to learn what the people were queuing up for.

"What's available?" he asked an emaciated woman whose face revealed no life and little hope.

"Milk—so they say."

Petre raised his eyebrows. Milk was very scarce, even on the black market. His stomach turned. How could mothers keep their children strong without fresh milk?

Petre was reminded of his visit with Ceausescu and wondered if the dictator's blood pressure was high because he had to leave his wife, Elena, in charge of Romania next week. Student demonstrations in Transylvania were beginning to erupt. Instead of suppressing a revolution or giving the dissenters more freedoms, Ceausescu was fleeing the country. Was his blood sugar increasing with the thought that it was too risky to take his gold to Tehran?

In disgust, Petre left the line and continued walking. He kicked a stone, which hit an old man in another line. "What are you waiting here for?" Petre asked the peasant as he apologized for hitting his leg. The man hadn't felt the stone. His legs were numb from a lifetime of waiting in lines.

"Eggs." He shrugged. "The sign says each person can have two eggs."

Petre had nothing to say. He looked at the lines of people, who were nothing more than lifeless shells. He thought of the dead souls wandering in Hades without a coin, blocked by Cerberus, the three-headed dog, unable to die in peace.

A teenage girl carrying a package approached him. She put the blanketed bundle to his face and said, "Please, take it." He heard a cry and thought it was a kitten, but when the blanket fell back, he realized it was an infant. The face was spotted red and oozing with pus.

Petre shook his head, and muttered "No." He moved away. His people had been reduced to giving away their babies dying of typhus. He was determined to change this—as a doctor and humanitarian.

He walked on, passing a building with broken windows. When he was a boy, before Ceausescu's reign of terror, the buildings had been painted the yellow of the Habsburg flag, sunny and proud.

Though the colors were drab now, the architecture still reminded him of Vienna. Every six months for the past nineteen years, Ceausescu had sent him to Vienna for medical meetings. Petre loved those trips. He felt alive as he travelled west, where the air wasn't polluted and flowers grew everywhere.

The dictator, plagued by diabetes, wanted to make sure that his doctor stayed up to date on the latest medications and treatments. To risk his doctor escaping to the West was a gamble for Ceausescu, but Petre had never thought to defect: his work wasn't finished.

He had used the privilege to travel to meet up with undercover agents from his network. They were working for the Americans, Russians, British, and French, who were giving him updated information. They all agreed: Ceausescu had to be eliminated.

They'd meet in a café, sitting at separate tables, only acknowledging each other with a glance. Messages were left inside a newspaper on a random park bench or in a garbage can. Codes and secrets were an everyday part of these medical meetings abroad.

The other benefit was he could maintain his CIA training. The physical aspect of this training was what he enjoyed the most. For twenty-four hours, he'd work with an operative outside Vienna, focusing on his level of timing and strength in a range of skills from grenade launching to martial arts.

After his day and night of physical training, Petre would walk through the city alone. He'd turn into side streets, alleyways, markets, abandoned buildings, and when he felt that no one was following him, he'd indulge in his favorite pleasure: wandering freely through the city, feeling its vibrancy.

Vienna was one of his favorite cities. He loved to follow the sidewalks along Vienna's main "Ring" where the squares of cement created a ladder pattern. As he walked, he imagined he was climbing the ladder, never stopping.

On the way to his hotel, still not tired, he'd buy a stack of newspapers written in German, English, and French. He'd read the papers through the night, always thinking of ways to overturn the evil in his country.

Petre wanted the vibrant red and purple flowers he saw in Vienna for his people, he wished for the same manicured gardens. He wanted them to have the same music he heard in the parks, the same joy in being alive. Most of all, he wanted to see Romanian children playing and laughing like the children in protected gardens of the Western world.

That was Vienna, and now he was in Bucharest. In only a couple of hours of walking through the Romanian city, Petre had seen his country's version of Homer's Hell.

He continued walking on Victoriei Street and passed the Hotel Plaza Athenée. Looking in the window, he saw a group of men he knew well; they were engaged in animated conversation. The table was full of food, although it was not yet lunch time: two bottles of champagne, a bottle of scotch, a large bowl of black caviar, a dozen hard-boiled eggs, tomatoes, cucumbers, cheese—foods found only in most Romanians' dreams.

Two young blonde girls, heavily made up, approached the men at the table. The body language of the men changed. Everyone laughed. The women sat down. Petre hesitated, then waved at his colleagues, smiled, and entered the hotel.

He sat down and joined the group. He had known all the men of Ceausescu's inner circle for years. There was Ion Raceppa, head of the Secret Service, Sergiu Iannade, Minister of Finance, Mircea Constatanu, Minister of Foreign Affairs, and Mihai Manescu, the dictator's chief advisor. Petre had to laugh and drink with them from time to time or they wouldn't trust him.

He poured himself a glass of champagne, took a slice of toast and spread Beluga caviar on it. He was hungry. He listened to their chatter, smiled, and then decided to join their frivolity by entertaining them with a story about having spent the previous evening in the same dining room.

"Some others from our circle arranged a private belly dancing show with several Gypsy women. They pushed me to dance with the prettiest one. Then each of our four comrades put a hundred-dollar bill in her underpants and pushed me into her. I had to dance."

They all laughed.

After more of the story, another tale, and more bantering, Petre stood up and excused himself. "Sorry, friends. I must return to my apartment."

"Stay," one of the women implored him. "You're so handsome. We've just met. I can prove you'll like me."

"I'm sure you can. Another time, but not on a Sunday." He winked at her and she smiled.

"Is the person you're meeting as beautiful as me?"

"Not possible," he answered, and kissed her hand Romanian style. He said goodbye to his so-called friends, kissed the two women cheek-to-cheek, and left.

Petre used three keys to open the three separate locks of his apartment door. As soon as he entered the marble entry, he smelled the fragrance of dozens of roses. They had been placed by his housekeeper in vases scattered throughout the spacious apartment. He walked over to one of the vases and smelled the flowers. He remembered the French singer, Gilbert Bécaud's popular song, and hummed the words, *"L'important c'est la rose..."* Then he walked toward his large terrace, unbolted and opened the door to let in the winter air from Ioanid Park.

He put his keys on a shelf in the library next to his favorite marble statue of Brancusi's *Flying Fish* and walked from the wood-paneled library to the decorated living room, turning on several Baccarat crystal chandeliers and opening all the windows in the room.

Ileyesco hates the cold, he thought, *and he dislikes that my new*

*apartment is grander than his. I won't offer him anything to eat. Just
something to drink. It'll go to his head and give me an edge.*

He put on the music by pressing a button on the wall. He
dimmed the chandelier, took a bottle of Dom Perignon champagne
from the bar, two champagne flutes, and a crystal bucket for ice.

Luxury and affluence in a poor country. Petre's privileged lifestyle in return for being Ceausescu's doctor, his reward for
keeping the dictator strong. Yet the sculptures, the champagne,
and the finery meant nothing to Petre. He had been happier in two
rooms years ago with Anca. This was his role now: to seem to be
like everyone else in Ceausescu's inner circle. He had to continue
acting and setting the stage.

He went to his bedroom, put away his comfortable, old peasant
coat, and took out a silk lounging robe with a matching ascot that
he had bought in Vienna a few months ago. He had been there
with his daughter, Sandi, who was soon to start college at Yale. He
hoped the silk robe would make Ian Ileyesco jealous.

The security guard rang from downstairs. Petre answered, then
moved to the front door to greet his guest.

He heard Ileyesco at the door. "Come in, my dear friend. I'm
pleased you're here."

"It's been a couple of weeks since I've seen you," Ileyesco said.

"We've both been busy."

The two men stood next to each other for several seconds
without talking. Petre was a head taller than his rival, and more
strongly built, with broader shoulders and more muscular arms.
Ian Ileyesco was thin and pale, and wore wire-framed eyeglasses
that gave him a bookish look. He was the same age as Petre, but
had graying hair and a receding hairline. Yet his dark eyes shone
with a fierce determination. He was not a man to be trifled with.

"How about a drink?" Petre asked. "We have a lot to celebrate."

"Yes, one drink, but no celebrations, not yet. It's too soon and I
haven't had lunch yet."

"Right," Petre nodded.

They sat down with a glass of champagne. "Any news from Moscow?" Petre asked.

Ceausescu had sent Ileyesco out of Bucharest five months before in July when Gorbachev had visited. Ceausescu didn't trust either of them and wanted to prevent their direct contact. Knowing that Ileyesco spoke Russian, had studied in Moscow, and had befriended Gorbachev during his time there, Ceausescu had been sure to marginalize Ileyesco since the summer. The truth was, he suspected that Ileyesco was working with the Russians to overthrow him and Ceausescu was scheming when would be the right time to get rid of Ileyesco. In fact, he had even spoken to Petre about it while he was being examined.

"I've been in communication with Gorbachev," Ileyesco said. "He has proposed that I'll stay in Bucharest to lead the revolution from the capital. You're to stay in the countryside, in Timisoara, with Reverend Mokess. You'll start the revolution from there away from the international press, and I'll finish it here, with the Romanian press."

Petre didn't answer. He tried to appear as if he agreed, but in reality, he was reflecting that he'd be in Timisoara and start the revolution there, but he'll be at a disadvantage by not being in Bucharest. Ileyesco wanted to get the press for himself.

Petre realized that while he was thinking about this, his silence was making Ileyesco feel uncomfortable. The unease was making his competitor talk more.

"Gorbachev has arranged for some of our generals to turn against Ceausescu. I believe they will come over to our side," Ileyesco said.

"Which generals?" Petre asked.

"Stamkulesco. Ceausescu trusts him. Stamkulesco and I will take the dictator and his wife from Bucharest by helicopter. At first, they won't protest. Then we'll take them to an army barracks in a small town that we control."

"Who's *we*?"

"Me and our comrades in Bucharest."

"And then?"

"We'll put him on trial for crimes against humanity. He'll be executed with Elena. I'll give word that they shouldn't shoot the dictator above his chest, so we can use his face for the press and photos. They can shoot Elena between the eyes, for all I care. Many times."

"And then?"

"*Then?* No more Ceausescu."

Petre didn't comment. He didn't trust Ileyesco and the followers he had chosen in Bucharest. He thought again that being in Timisoara would be a disadvantage for himself as well.

"Let the people decide who will be the next leader," Ileyesco said, apparently annoyed that Petre was reticent to talk with him aside from a few words. "The people need a strong leader. What do the *people* know about governing on their own?"

"We should have a clearer plan," Petre stated calmly. "You can't start a revolution, enflame the people, and give them nothing afterwards. A political void is dangerous."

Petre knew that Ileyesco's vision was different than his. Ileyesco didn't believe in transforming the communist government into a democratic one: He believed in socialism with one-man leadership. Freedom was not his goal. Human rights, according to Ileyesco, weren't right for everyone.

"I know what you're thinking," Ileyesco commented. "You've been influenced by Reagan, Thatcher, and the Pope. Democracy won't work in Romania. It's nothing but a dream, an ideal that the Romanians, like the Russians, know nothing about."

"People know about freedom instinctively," Petre stated. "What's unnatural is to chain human beings down like animals."

Ileyesco finished his drink and held out his glass for another one. "When are you going to Timisoara?"

"This afternoon."

"I'll let you get ready." Ileyesco put down his empty glass, went to the closet, took his coat, and walked to the front door. "Good luck. I'll be in my office for the next few weeks. I have a bed there. Keep in touch with me."

Petre wanted to have the last word. He wasn't finished with his opponent, but he'd wait. For now, he gave him a smile and a handshake.

Petre walked over to the terrace door, closed it, and shut all the windows. He turned off the lights, took off his silk robe and ascot, and went to his bedroom closet to reach for his old sweater. He sat down on the couch in the library to think.

Clearly, Ileyesco was warning him. They were now open competitors, each one with a different interpretation of a post-Ceausescu era. Petre wanted a Western-style democracy with multiparty elections and the removal of dictatorial institutions like the secret police and the espionage agency. He wanted an independent jurisdiction, especially to stop corruption. He had firmly believed that corruption was too prevalent in the country. Ileyesco simply envisioned replacing Ceausescu with himself, then continuing with the same one-man, corrupt system and the same chains for the people—his idea of an enlightened dictatorship.

He knew he'd have to be careful. Petre had set the stage this morning for a duel. Perhaps it had been a mistake to make Ileyesco angry.

Petre stood up, went to his closet again, took out his old coat and his ragged woolen scarf. He wouldn't allow himself to be derailed by anyone. He had his own motives, and his own ambitions.

Before he turned out the lights in his room, his eyes caught a row of photos at his night table: Anca, pregnant with Sandi before she left; Sandi at ten years old, when he took the photo the first time she had visited him in Europe; Sandi at eleven, at the first fencing tournament she had won; and Sandi with Argus, his dog that he had to give to his best friend, Eugen, while he traveled. They were pictures from his past—a good past with a beautiful woman. But, she was a woman who didn't trust him anymore, and didn't want him. Her letter had told him so, when she had signed their divorce papers, ten years ago.

He tightened his scarf and went out to walk toward the train station. It's going to be colder in Timisoara, he thought, despite all the fire and guns. I'll start the uprising and reward the people with freedom. I'll do what I know is destined: overthrow a pitiless dictator, the keeper of Romania's Hades, and I will lead the people toward freedom.

5

NEW YORK CITY

IMAGES of the past continued to plague Anca, even from her kitchen in New York.

She and Dory left the Gypsy's cottage without speaking. Looking at the ground, she said to herself, "We need more vaccines and tetracycline. This epidemic isn't ending quickly."

When she returned to the clinic, she heard Petre yelling at a huge man —far taller than him and twice as broad. She moved to the corner of the room and studied the man's face. She stared at his pockmarked skin and his chipped front teeth.

"I won't do what you say," came Petre's unflinching voice. As Anca watched Petre, she realized his refusal to back down from doing what was right was what she loved about him. The man was yelling, "I decide who gets the medicines. How dare you think you have more authority than me." He was ready to strike Petre with his walking stick when Anca bolted from her corner, running into the behemoth, making it look accidental.

"Oh, excuse me," she said curtly. "Are you a patient?"

"*I am the secretary of the party committee for the entire province of Transylvania.*" He slapped his stick on the desk next to her. "*I was talking to the doctor.*" Then he stopped talking, as he realized she was pointing the way out.

"*The lady is also a doctor,*" Petre said. He stepped up next to Anca and put his arm around her to calm her temper. "*She is my wife.*"

"*Then I will address you both. These orders are from the top. No typhus vaccine or antibiotics are to be given to anyone who is not a Party member. No one else.*"

"*That is unheard of,*" Petre retorted. "*The medicines are mine.*"

The secretary spoke very clearly. "*There are no privately owned medicines in a communist country.*" He moved to the refrigerator. "*Give me the keys.*"

Petre had no choice but to turn them over. Anca looked at Petre, trying to catch his eye, but he avoided her gaze.

The Party boss put the glass vials in his pocket. Before leaving he declared, "*These are now state property.*"

Petre waited until he heard the front door slam. He turned to Anca with a boyish grin on his face. "*Don't worry. They're placebos. I'm still waiting for someone to bring the real stuff.*"

Anca sat down on a broken chair. She put her head in her hands.

"*Petre,*" she whispered, "*he'll realize we tricked him and take revenge. He'll put us in prison. What kind of future do we have in this hell?*"

She cried the tears she had held back all morning. Petre knelt and buried his nose in her stomach swollen with their love. Softly, he rocked her in his arms and whispered, "*Yes, my love, yes, I'll get you out.*"

He held her as long as he could, knowing he'd have to let her go. "*I'll get you both out.*"

Anca wiped the hurt from her eyes. So many years without him. Turning her thoughts back to the newspaper, she tried to erase

Petre from her mind and to focus on what she was reading. Where was Romania's nuclear facility? How could it be denuclearized? The Americans wouldn't leave it intact knowing that Ceausescu was working with Arafat, Gaddafi, Saddam, Rafsanjani, and Kim Il-Sung. They needed someone they trusted—someone the people would follow.

As she was trying to piece together the puzzle, the phone rang again. This time, she pounced on the receiver. "Speak!"

"Anca..." A woman's voice—muted and far away. "It's me, Evdochia. Pine trees are in trouble."

"What do you mean?"

A click. Anca could feel her heart thumping like a war drum.

"Speak to me!" she yelled into the phone receiver. "Pine trees in trouble? What does that mean?" The line went dead.

She sat down, trying to decipher the message. Clearly, her friend was warning her of trouble. All Anca could see before her was Evdochia, her Gypsy friend whose baby boy Anca had saved. She hadn't seen or heard from Evdochia in nineteen years. Evdochia, the leader of the Gypsies, with long black wavy hair and eyes as shiny as black diamonds—a tall, broadly built woman, strong in body and soul.

Anca remembered her one-room cottage. She smiled, thinking of the small garden where several times a week after dinner, dozens of Gypsies and peasants came to hear Evdochia's prophecies, as she read their palms, tea leaves, or coffee grains. Sometimes when Anca made a house call in the Gypsy camp, she'd pass by Evdochia's garden and linger a while, but Anca didn't dare extend her palm to the Gypsy. No, Anca was a woman of science, a doctor who believed in antibiotics, not tea leaves.

The morning sun entered the kitchen windows and Anca moved away from the glare. Picking up a pen and paper, she began writing out a to-do list, but she was distracted and went to the stove to warm up the coffee. Mesmerized by the flame, she was taken back to Evdochia and remembered how the Gypsy had begun her séances by lighting a candle. How had the Gypsy gotten her telephone number, and what did the warning mean? The last time she had seen Evdochia, the Gypsy had taken her hand and kissed it. "Thank you for saving my son. I hope one day I will be able to help you." Had her telephone message been linked to the fulfillment of that promise?

———————

Petre had criticized their friendship. "You're bringing too much attention to yourself," he had complained.

"Too much attention? What does that mean?"

"Don't go to the Gypsy camp. You're being watched and your friendship with them puts you in danger. You're taking care of them, giving them antibiotics and food."

She feared what he'd say next.

"You can be arrested. You'll have to escape."

"Escape?"

"Alec told me there's a defective tractor. He'll hide you in it and use it as a ruse to move you out of the country. No one will know."

"No. We'll find another way."

"Why are you so stubborn? It's the chance of a lifetime. You have to think of the baby now, not just yourself."

"I won't leave without you."

"Alec's tractor deals are coming to an end. In another couple of months, he'll make another defective tractor for my escape. He has a secret system to detach some fine wires needed to start the motor. He's the only one who knows the system. He's the only one who can do it."

6

NEW HAVEN, CONNECTICUT

> *It is a wise child that knows its father.*
>
> — HOMER, *THE ODYSSEY*, BOOK 1

SANDRA WAS ALONE in her dorm room at Yale. She had just finished studying and was getting ready to begin her day. Her routine was tight and disciplined: rising at 6:00 to memorize her French vocabulary and chemistry formulas, then reviewing the day's homework and classes. She did her schoolwork in the morning so that she'd be free in the afternoons to fence. She had promised her mother she'd divide her time equally between studies and sports.

Sandra stopped reading for a moment and put her French grammar aside. She glanced at her mother's picture framed on her desk. She thought about calling her, despite the early hour, to discuss their Christmas plans. Sandra knew Anca had a habit of rising early to read the newspaper before going to work.

She nibbled on an apple and dialed the number. When she heard her mother's frantic voice, "Speak! Who are you?" Sandra knew something was wrong.

"Mom, are you okay?"

"Oh, Sandi," Anca responded in relief. "Did you call me before?"

"No. You sound weird. Is something wrong?"

"No, nothing. I'm glad it's you. How are you, *darling*?"

"Everything's cool."

The girl's American slang contrasted with her mother's Romanian accent. Anca had never lost the roll of her *r*'s.

"Where are you?"

"In my room, studying, then going to breakfast. Did I wake you?"

"No," Anca answered. Then, in a more controlled voice, she asked, "How's school?"

"First snow of the year. Can't use my bike. Walking slows me down."

"They'll clear it by tomorrow."

"Every minute counts. I'm up at six to prepare classes for the day and review from the day before. The dorm is quiet then and my mind is fresh. Breakfast at eight…"

"Don't you eat anything from six to eight?"

"I munch on fruit."

"Umm." The doctor in Anca wasn't satisfied.

"After breakfast, I have three classes in a row."

"Isn't that too much without a break?"

"Nope, it works out. Lunch at noon. On to the library until three and then to the gym until nine with a quick break for dinner."

"Any tournaments I can go to?"

"Mom, don't you remember? How can you forget? Saturday at Princeton—the Ivies. We're meeting Mica there. The twins are also fencing."

"I've been a little preoccupied," Anca said, and didn't elaborate as to why.

Sandra continued chatting. "Listen to this. They wrote a long article about me in the college newspaper with photos of me fencing."

"Really?"

"The writer said I'm Olympic material. Isn't that cool? You know the pictures you took of me with your old camera for my high school yearbook? I submitted them for the Freshman Directory, and they landed in the hands of a journalist. He wants to do a feature article on me and take some other photos of me fencing."

"Your father gave me the camera for our first anniversary. I always wondered why and how he got hold of a Kodak in Romania. 'Friends,' he said, but he never finished his explanation."

"Well, anyway," interrupted Sandra, "Not only is he going to write the article, but he's also going to pay me $300 for posing for the fencing photos. Isn't that cool?"

"That's a lot of money. For what newspaper?"

"He didn't say."

"What's his name?"

"Not important. What's important is the press. If I want to go to Yale Law, these are the things that will get the attention of the admissions committee."

"Wait a minute. You're at Yale to study. That's why I work so hard to pay the bills. You're not there just to fence. You promised to give equal time to each, remember, equal hours, equal passion."

"Mom, I'm very grateful for what you do for me, but I can't help but feel that fencing is more exciting than studying."

"I've spent my whole life studying. I still do. I find it very exciting," Anca said.

"Well, I spoke to this guy on the phone for half an hour. He sounded legit. He wants to meet me."

"How do you know he's not a pervert?"

"Oh, Mom, please. He must be connected somehow with the college. How else would he have gotten the directory?"

"I don't like this," Anca commented.

"He knew I was a fencer. Above all, he said he likes my 'exotic' looks."

Sandra knew that people found her intriguing, and she enjoyed the interest. Even though she had her mother's slanted eyes and high cheekbones, she resembled her father more. In Romania, he was often taken for a Scandinavian. Like him, she was tall and slender, with blonde hair and blue eyes.

"Take a young man with you," Anca insisted. "Better yet, speak to your college master and ask him to check out this journalist before you go."

"Oh, Mom, he's not going to rape me in broad daylight."

"Where's his office?"

"Well, it's not exactly an office." Sandra hesitated. "It's his studio, on Chapel Street, in the middle of town."

"Don't go."

Sandra was getting annoyed. She had only been at college for one semester, but she'd seen enough of other students to know that not all parents were so uptight. Hearing her mother's alarm, she came up with a compromise. "I'll take a guy from the fencing team. We can fence together for the photo shoot."

Sandra understood that Anca's past shadowed her present. Still, she resented her mother's pull on her. She wanted so much to be independent and to make her own decisions. "You know, Mom, I'm not a child anymore. I shouldn't have told you any of this." Then she said in a calmer tone, "I promise I won't go alone."

Somewhere in the back of her mind, Sandra understood that the situation seemed a little weird. She didn't see any need to be alarmed. She prided herself on being more controlled than her mother—more like her father. She liked identifying with him, especially since he had been absent most of her life, with the exception of the time they vacationed together in Europe. He had told her that he had always loved sports also. Swimming, he said, had saved his life.

Anca asked Sandra for the journalist's name, address, telephone number, and time of appointment. When Sandra called him Henry Brown, Anca said, "Oh, come on. That name sounds too common. I'm calling the police."

"No!" Sandra yelped. She didn't want her mother's fears to ruin this opportunity for her. Then, trying to change the subject, Sandra began talking about their Christmas plans. After a few *okays* and *maybes,* Sandra added, "Sorry, Mom, gotta go now."

Before saying goodbye, she promised to call the next day about "Henry Brown."

After she hung up, Sandra took a quick shower and decided to leave her hair wet despite the cold, so the strands would straggle in the air. She loved feeling free.

It was Sunday and she had the whole day to herself to do what she enjoyed the most. Unlike other Sundays, she had no fencing tournament, so she could stay at Whitney Gym all day and fence one bout after another. She loved to practice over and over, improving her timing and rhythm, making her moves natural as if her fencing and breathing were one.

As Sandra left the dining room and crossed the quad, she put a tape into her Walkman and enjoyed her stroll past Beinecke Library toward the gym. It was still snowing. White flakes covered the quad and landed on the gray gothic stones of the buildings like feathers flying with the wind.

At each covered archway, Sandra paused to wipe the snow off her face and to read the announcements of college events. She breathed in the smell of the fresh snow mixing with evergreen trees and swayed to the rhythm of music beating in her ears. Noticing a table of used books, she joined a group of students leafing through them.

She picked up the biggest book on the stand—*Medicine in Europe Before Antibiotics* and remembered her mother's story of a typhus epidemic in Romania during the sixties, an epidemic that lasted months. Her father had somehow gotten tetracycline from the States to treat their patients in Transylvania. No one knew how he had arranged it, not even her mother.

Sandra put down the book. *Medicine isn't for me,* she thought. *My mom does enough for both of us.*

She continued looking through the books. A large red volume caught her eye—*American Sports.* She turned to the table of contents: *Archery, Baseball,* and *Basketball,* but no *Fencing.* It's probably considered European. She skimmed the list of contents to the bottom and read, *Swimming,* and thought of her father. He had been Romania's Junior Champion in breaststroke at fifteen.

"Sports," he had told her, "are important to teach us how to lose and then start again. We always need a goal and the hope to win."

She remembered he had told her that his earliest memory was when he was five years old. He was vacationing at the Black Sea with his parents and had wandered away from them. He was searching for shells and accidentally fell. The waves caught him and he'd gone under the water. His mother heard him yelling, and she ran towards his voice. She jumped into the sea and swam to save him.

"After that," he told Sandi, "she taught me how to swim. I was happy that I won my first championship before she died. I wanted my mother to have my medal."

Petre had been very reserved when talking about his parents, but sometimes, when he saw something that reminded him of them, he'd share his past with Sandi.

"I was an only child and loved my parents a lot."

"Like me." She smiled.

"Yes." He took her hand and squeezed it. "My mother had been a champion swimmer in her youth and trained with me every morning until I made the national team. We'd swim in our town pool from six in the morning till eight. Then she'd walk me to school and she'd go to work. She was the chief librarian in Cluj, Transylvania.

"My father was a physician, an internist, and taught at the medical school. Everyone respected him. It was natural for him to get involved with the anti-communists. He was a true humanist. Eventually they got him. They gave him a *Radu*."

"What's that?"

"A code word to indicate his office or home had been irradiated by the communists. They poisoned the air, and they poisoned him.

"I suffered with him, watching him die, as if he was melting away from me—leaving me forever—and I wasn't able to save him. It was horrible."

Sandi remembered her father had stopped talking for several minutes. When he spoke again, it was in a different tone. "That's when I swore revenge."

"Did they find out who did it, or put them in jail?"

"Who could put the communist government in jail? But that's what drives me to do what I do. No government should poison their people. Not even with lies."

Sandi was silent.

"That horrible act offered me an opportunity, nonetheless. I defected then, right after I won a swimming tournament in Vienna. My father's friends helped me get to the States. Death bred rebirth."

Sandi loved her father, respected him, and wished that one day she could help her parents get back together. Then she'd have her father all the time. They'd be a family.

She finished skimming the chapter about different swimming strokes, moved on to another table, and there she saw a book with a bright blue cover—*Dr. Spy*.

She turned to the first page and read the prologue: "This is the story of a doctor who understands man's inner secrets and uses his medical knowledge as a camouflage."

Sandra thought again about her father and couldn't help but wonder if he was a "doctor-spy." If he was, who was he working for? She wondered if her mother knew.

The one thing Sandra understood was that her mother had never spoken against her father. On the contrary, Anca had raised Sandra to be proud of her father and had defended his need to remain in Romania.

By contrast, one of her mother's closest friends, Cristina, a fashion designer who lives in Paris, had always been critical of him. "He should have never let a pregnant woman attempt to escape alone," she had said.

Anca was more forgiving. "One day we'll know why he did it."

Sandra thought back to the trips she and her father had taken together, just the two of them, a few times a year when she had a school vacation, ever since she was ten years old. Her mother would drive her to the airport, check her in at the airline counter, and then a flight hostess would put a string around her neck with a printed sign, UNACCOMPANIED MINOR. Sandra would be watched throughout the trip until her father picked her up at the final destination.

Her father chose to meet her in Vienna or Budapest when she didn't have school and he had a medical conference. They'd tour the city, walking for hours, speaking Romanian like it was their secret language. He'd explain to her why he was traveling to medical meetings abroad, claiming he was learning from colleagues about new advances in endocrinology. He never said anything about conferring with colleagues on political matters.

In the past year, as he realized she was no longer a child, he'd share with her what was in his heart, his conflicts and struggles, why he'd chosen to stay in Romania despite his loving her and her mother so much.

"Freedom," he'd tell her, "is a gift from God. I hope that one day, I can give freedom to my people."

───────

"I'll buy this book," Sandra said to the student in charge and put *Dr. Spy* in her backpack. As she was making room for the book, she leaned against the stone building and took off her Walkman. When she looked up, a black car had stopped directly in front of her. A young man with a shaved head, dressed in black, poked his head out of the car. He was crude looking and stared at her angrily. Then he threw a small bottle of liquid at her. "For you and your mother."

As the bottle shattered on the snowy ground, smoke blackened the entire area and the crowd standing around the books, scattered. The car zoomed away. A jogger emptied his water bottle on the flames.

"What was that about?" a student asked.

"Must have been acid," a girl commented as she examined the smoky-fiery area that melted the snow.

An older man kicked the broken bottle. More smoke and a sizzling sound. "Does anyone know anything about this incident or that guy?" he asked, turning his attention to Sandra.

"What guy?" she answered, terrified. "I've only been in New Haven a few months. I don't know many people here. I'm just a freshman." She thought right away of the phone conversation with her mother and her warning.

"I'm Professor Butler, master of Payne College and chairman of the Department of History," the older man identified himself. "What's your name?"

"Sandra Ilianu." She tried to nonchalantly dry her jeans, but she noticed there were black burn marks and holes in the denim. Her skin felt itchy.

"Can I have your telephone number and address?" Butler asked, taking out a pad and pencil.

Sandra was still shaken and felt disoriented. She didn't want to believe her mother's suspicions. "Thank you, but I'm fine," she said, avoiding his gaze. She walked away.

"Be careful," he called after her. "I've written down your name. I hope there's no more trouble. Also, I have to tell you that I'm obliged to report this incident to security."

Confused and upset, Sandra didn't say anything. All she wanted was to be alone. Retracing her steps, she walked back to the quad, sat down on a bench and stretched out her jeans. Taking a handkerchief, she wiped her puffy, red skin.

Why had the man shouted, "For you and your mother"? Sandra couldn't help but wonder if there was a connection between this incident and the journalist's interest in her. Did her mother know something she wasn't telling her? It was probably why she had been so worried on the phone.

Sandra was prone to rebel, but she was no fool. Both of her parents had warned her repeatedly about the secret police. She had promised her mother to be careful, and to take the strongest fencer with her to the interview. She didn't want to cancel the appointment. She was as stubborn as her mother.

When she arrived at the gym, she adjusted the earphones that had fallen to her neck, and then changed her mind and put them away in her backpack. Touching the book, *Dr. Spy*, she whispered to herself, "I'd better not tell my mom. She'll insist I report this to the Yale authorities. I'd better be careful."

7

NEW YORK CITY

ANCA STRETCHED in her blue négligée and turned on her tape deck. Humming Enescu's *Romanian Rhapsody*, she lingered in bed with her eyes closed, drifting along with the music.

As she was falling back asleep, the phone rang. *It's probably just another prank call,* she thought. She tried to ignore it. *Or, maybe it's Sandra calling back, telling me she won't go to the journalist's studio after all.* She decided to pick it up after all.

"Anca?" came the faraway voice. "I can't hear you."

"Who's speaking?" She was afraid it was the Gypsy with another cryptic message.

"It's me, Cristina. I'm calling from Paris."

Relieved, Anca sat down on her bed. She had some time before meeting Mica at Marina's for brunch.

"*Cristina, draga. Ce mai faci?* How are you? I haven't heard from you in a week. I called you at home, even at the showroom. One of your assistants said you were traveling. No one seemed to know where."

"I came home last night. I was in Vienna and Nice, talking to investors."

"You still need a challenge?"

"This is the last one. The most important."

"What is it? Tell me." Anca always enjoyed hearing about Cristina's work. Fashion design was a different world from medicine. As Cristina chattered away, Anca turned the music down. She sat down on the green club chair next to her desk and abandoned herself to her friend's words.

"*Ma chère, écoute-moi,* I'm giving you a present: a first-class plane ticket to Paris."

"Thank you, but I promised to spend Christmas with Sandra. Petre told her he can't be with her this year. Why, I don't know."

"I have one for Sandra, too. Don't say no." Cristina was all business. It was clear she was used to getting her way. "Besides, I need you."

"What happened?"

"First, say yes."

"Tell me," coaxed Anca in a tone she had used with her friend since they were both thirteen years old.

The Four Musketeers—Anca, Cristina, Marina, and Mica. "One for all and all for one," they had sworn.

"I want you to be my bridesmaid. I'm getting married." She announced it almost solemnly, without the joy of her previous banter.

Anca paused and then laughed. "I wouldn't miss it for the world."

She knew Eugen well, her friend's partner of twenty years. He had been Petre's best friend since they were in high school; only Petre had chosen to remain in Romania when they had all left. Even though Cristina and Eugen had been a couple for as long as she could remember, whenever Anca went to visit Cristina in Paris, Eugen was never there. He was always traveling.

"When's the wedding?"

"New Year's Eve. Three weeks from today. I'm designing something for you, Mica, Marina, and Sandra to wear."

Cristina had taken care of every detail, just as she always did.

"Why now? Will marriage change your life?" Anca was curious as to why Cristina and Eugen were marrying after so many years of living together.

"No. I won't let it," Cristina answered as if she had just realized what she was doing. "You know, freedom is the most important thing for me. Isn't that why the four of us left Romania?"

"That's a different kind of freedom. Marriage may put limits on you in other ways."

"Eugen knows that if he pressures me, I'll retreat and shut him out. Anyway, why should he or anything change because of a certificate?"

"You're right. Don't you feel guilty that you can't give yourself completely to him?"

"If I could, I wouldn't be me—the person he loves."

"Or you'll suffer?" added Anca, thinking about her own pain when Petre couldn't give himself completely to her.

"Perhaps I want to suffer."

"What?" The doctor in Anca jumped.

"Odd, but I need that push and pull inside of me. Like a ball of fire—a force. That's what makes me go to the drawing board and design. Then a calm comes over me, and for a moment, I feel at peace."

"You're lucky you have your art." Anca compared that to the fact that she had her medicine. When she helped a child feel less pain and then got a smile of thanks, she felt satisfied; even happy.

"Still," Cristina said, "I don't want peace all the time. I'll lose my drive."

Anca thought again of Petre. *Was he driven like Cristina—driven by his humanitarian vision, but also in part by ambition?* She wondered why she was thinking so much of him today.

"What about Mark?" Cristina asked. "Why don't you marry him? He's proposed so many times."

Mark had not only been Anca's boyfriend-partner for ten years, but was also her colleague at New York Hospital. Last year, he had become the chief of pediatrics.

"I don't know if I love him enough to get married," Anca said in all honesty. "Once was enough."

"Aha! You can't free yourself from Petre. Why don't you give the old fox a call? Whenever I see him, the first thing he asks me is about you. He told me he's tried to have a conversation with you when he phones Sandra, but you refuse to talk, other than to discuss Sandi's vacation plans. He says you don't even answer his letters."

"It's true. You know, ten years ago, I filed divorce papers. I realized he'd never join me in New York, so I thought I might as well be *legally* free. I even attached a letter." She took a deep breath, remembering that letter. "Life went on," she whispered, and then with a stronger voice, asked, "Why take his side now? You always blamed him for letting me escape alone."

"I don't know. Petre has many faces. There's an idealistic side that I admire."

How ironic life is, Anca mused to herself. *I thought Mark would make me happy because he needs me. I was happier loving a man who didn't need me at all.*

"Your talking about Petre reminds me of something strange that happened to me last March when I was visiting you in Paris."

"What? You never told me about it."

"Probably because I was ashamed that I didn't act, or that I lost my chance."

"What are you talking about?" Cristina was surprised. So unlike her friend—a woman of action, and so very determined.

"I was walking on the promenade along the Seine, going

toward Notre Dame. It was a cloudy day with thick fog covering the bridges. The Seine seemed to fold into the sky, when I saw a tall, blond man crossing the Pont des Arts to the other side. I was sure it was Petre, even in the fog. I followed him.

"Suddenly, my heart started pounding and my legs stiffened. They got so heavy. I wanted to run toward him, but I was barely able to walk.

"It started to rain. He put on his hat, raised his collar, and walked quickly into a small street. The rain came down in torrents. I took out my umbrella, opened it, and in that second, I lost him. I lost him to the rain and to the fog. I couldn't find him. I couldn't see him at all.

"When I returned to New York the next day, I decided to call him. It was his birthday, so I had an excuse.

"I remember his birthday the last time we were together. The Gypsies gave me fresh eggs, milk, and flour to make him a cake. He was so surprised.

"'Where did you get these treasures?' he laughed.

"We celebrated, the two of us, making love on the cold floor while rolling in the warm bear rug."

Anca stopped talking. She took a deep breath, trying not to cry.

Cristina was silent for several seconds, and then said, "Listen, would you like me to arrange a meeting with you and Petre at my place in Paris? I've asked you a dozen times—maybe now is the right time?"

"No. No."

There was another pause between the two friends.

"Anca, my dear," Cristina whispered, "we'll talk more about this in a few weeks when we're together. For now, according to what you've been telling me, I'd suggest you try to distract yourself. Keep busy," she advised. "The best remedy is to get involved in another project."

"I am. Actually, that's one of the problems." Anca's voice faltered. "Recently, I've been doing some political work—reviewing articles for the *Times* and broadcasting messages over Voice of America—secret messages to Romanians in Eastern Europe. I think someone may be trying to threaten me to get me to stop. Most of all, the problem is Sandra. I'm afraid someone is trying to harm me by getting to her."

Anca stopped talking, worried that she had said too much and that her phone might be bugged. But she couldn't hold in one final thought. "I sense something very important is going on in Romania. I can't figure out what it is, or why someone would want to get to me or Sandi."

"Speak to Alec. He may have some friends in Washington who have information. You should get protection." Cristina sounded as if she knew for sure something was smoldering. "Promise?"

"Maybe I'll see him at Marina's today. I'm meeting Mica there. I'll speak to them both."

"You may not be safe. Get Sandra out of New Haven. And you, get out of New York City. I'd invite you here, but you're not safe with me either—not yet."

Anca wanted to ask why *not yet*, but Cristina interrupted her. *"Ma chère,* I have an emergency meeting with my staff. I'll call you later. Plan *now* for your safety. Please be careful."

Anca hung up, turned out the lights in her bedroom, and went to the living room to her desk. She opened the bottom drawer where she found a copy of the letter she had written to Petre ten years ago, explaining why she wanted a divorce, and why she had decided to live her life without him.

The pages were yellowed. She remembered how she had labored writing them, hesitating after each paragraph, putting them away for days without finding her thoughts. And then, she'd try again—try to be rational, determined, and not cry. She didn't want to hurt him, even though he had hurt her.

She began to read it now. At first, she didn't remember what she had written, and she thought the words had come from someone else. Then moved, tears flowed down her cheeks. She read the letter while her innermost being broke with emotion:

Dear Petre,

This is very hard for me to write; and yet, I tell myself, I must. I must free myself from loving you. I must free myself from the past, so I can become stronger.

I will never forget how much I trusted you. Trusted you more than I trusted myself. Yet this trust has turned to sadness, and my love has twisted into pain.

We had wanted so much from life—to be together, to help the sick become well, to share what is good in life, to watch our daughter grow into a loving person. Now, after so many years without you, our paths have found different goals, which I can only ask of myself. No more of you.

In my quietest hours, you are no more within me, no longer near me. I am unspeakably alone. My feelings have taken a life without you, something I had never wanted. I have accepted this aloneness, and accepted living in a foreign country where you placed me without my consent. Yet this inner solitude has become a strength to connect me back to life—not with you, but because of you.

To have loved you and to have lost you has been very difficult for me. I have promised myself that I will not allow my past love to turn me bitter or resentful. For this reason, I want our daughter to grow up loving you, her father, and respecting your work and decisions, despite my hurt.

I want Sandi to understand that loving does not mean to lose oneself or to surrender oneself to the other. This you have taught me, even though it was not your intention. I have been obliged to stand alone, and this has given me opportunities to redefine who I am. I don't want Sandi to think that the great love I had for you was for naught. I want her to love her father as she loves her mother.

My only wish is that you discover your daughter, learn what she likes and dislikes, enjoy being with her, laugh with her. Spend time with her, and meet her where you can and when she has vacations. Talk to her of your dreams and goals so she will not judge you. Let her understand why you did what you did—to give freedom to her and to others so they can be free to love life.

She will need you, and I shall never prevent her from sharing her life with you. She is our gift—yours as well as mine. I will cooperate with you and your schedules to be with her.

I have to accept that I cannot have you, but that doesn't mean that Sandi cannot have her father.

Anca

Anca put the letter back in the drawer. Slowly, she turned out all the lights in her apartment. As she dressed for Marina's party, she tried not to think of Petre or her letter. She tried to change her thoughts, but she couldn't. Cristina's warnings, the Gypsy's phone call, the interest from Sandra's mysterious journalist—they all frightened her. There are no coincidences. She was receiving warnings—warnings that told her she'd have to take action, and quickly.

———

Anca lived on the corner of Madison Avenue and Eighty-ninth Street. She started walking south toward Marina's apartment, telling herself that the cool air would allow her to think more clearly. The wide avenue was empty, and it was a perfect day for a stroll.

As she crossed Madison Avenue and 86th Street, she saw a girl with fiery red hair and freckles all over her face who reminded her of Cristina when she was a schoolgirl. Cristina would plait her hair in pigtails and then she'd twist them on top of her head until she created a flaming crown of red. She wondered why she would marry Eugen after so many years of being together. What work did he really do?

Anca thought back to the first time she had met Cristina in Bucharest.

———

"Cristina! Cristina!" screamed the heavy Romanian woman dressed in black. "Wait for me. Don't run. I want to go in the church with you."

Before the girl could turn around and wait for her mother, she bumped into another girl who fell, striking her bare knees on a rock. Cristina bent down, helped the girl get up, and smiled at her as if she had saved her rather than pushed her down. "Your knees are bleeding."

"I'm fine. Bleeding is for weak kids."

"You're right," smiled the freckled face. "My name is Cristina. What's yours?"

Instinctively, Anca felt they'd have a lot to talk about.

"I'm going into the church to see the 'Crying Saint,'" Anca announced
to her new friend.

"Me too," and they ran together as the girl's mother shouted, *"Wait!"*

The "Crying Saint" was a painting on wood of Saint Irena, the
patron saint of peace. The painting rested on the main altar of the
Romanian Orthodox Church, surrounded by flowers, jewelry, and
gifts from parishioners. On the cheeks of the saint were two real
tears that didn't move. Anca had been told that the teardrops had
mysteriously appeared one day after the priest had secretly prayed
in his church.

The priest, Father Mihai Strancusi, was not allowed to hold
mass because religion was forbidden under communism, especially after Ceausescu had taken power. One morning at 6:00,
before the streets of Bucharest filled up with lines of people
waiting for food, he entered the abandoned sanctuary, threw
himself before the picture of Saint Irena and prayed for peace.

When he looked up, he saw two tears on the saint's face, tears
that never fell, never dried, never disappeared. The priest took it as
a sign from Christ and opened the chained doors. He ran into the
square and told the people that he had something more important
for them than food. The priest opened the doors and the people
entered the church, moving toward the picture in disbelief. Some
fainted, others cried, many shouted that it was a sign that freedom
would finally come to Romania.

The crowds kept coming to see the miracle.

The sick brought gifts and prayed for health.

The well brought flowers and prayed for peace.

The skeptics brought doubt, yet hoped for change.

One day, word spread to the presidential palace.

Soldiers in heavy boots came to inspect; police with rifles came to arrest. They tried to shut the doors, confiscate the gifts, remove the icon, stop the praying. The crowds wouldn't let them: they protested, they shouted, they fought. They wanted to believe. The Saint's tears were still there.

The "Crying Saint" became the symbol of peace and hope for Romania's future. Several weeks later, Ceausescu's soldiers came again. They chained the doors, arrested the priest, threw him in prison. Religion was forbidden to all.

8

NEW YORK CITY

WHEN ANCA ARRIVED at 68th Street and Fifth Avenue, she stopped before entering the building and searched in her pocketbook for her lipstick. The rectangular compact had been a gift from Marina. It resembled a cigarette case, made of soft, elegant Italian leather and containing two parts: one section with a small tube of mascara and mini brush; the other section with lipstick and mirror. "Lips and Lids," Marina had labeled her creation. She marketed it and pocketed a fortune.

A doorman wearing white gloves greeted Anca with a mechanical "Good day" and a detached "May I help you?", and Anca responded in the same indifferent manner. "Miss Marina Frigidescu." She continued in an equal tone, "I'm Dr. Rodescu."

Marina Frigidescu was a self-made woman. A beauty by birth and a chemist by education, she had come to New York from Romania twenty years ago at the age of twenty-two.

Anca, Marina, Cristina, and Mica had grown up together in their Transylvanian town. The "Four Musketeers" considered themselves to be family, and not having siblings, they were all closer than if they had been sisters.

It was Mica who took the role as anchor for all her friends. She had been the first of the four to leave Romania and did so on her own, in a daring escape. Mica's parents had been arrested for organizing an uprising against Ceausescu, and Mica realized that she'd be arrested next. Knowing that her father had hidden colored diamonds in their basement, she took the jewels and her bicycle and escaped in the middle of the night. From the Transylvanian-Hungarian border, she made her way to Budapest and months later, to her uncle in New York.

Mica sold three colored diamonds at Sotheby's for a fortune. Immediately afterwards, she dedicated herself to securing a way out of Romania for her parents.

Once the Romanian authorities learned that Mica was rich, they transferred her parents from jail to house arrest. Key politicians were eager to satisfy Mica's lawyers' request and her money for two exit visas.

It took Mica three years after she escaped to return to Transylvania in another daring feat to get her parents safely to America.

With the money from the sale of her colored diamonds, Mica also helped Marina and Cristina leave Romania for New York and Paris.

Since her school days, Mica had always been at the center of her friends, but it was for Anca that she had a special softness. Mica had always been protective of Anca, since the time they were thirteen years old. During communism, everyone was theoretically equal, but some were more deprived than others.

Anca's father, an engineering professor, had been arrested several times for opposing the government. Because of that, he was not allowed to continue teaching at the University. Her mother, often ill, had trouble readjusting socially and financially, and Anca had to take care of herself. It wasn't unusual that she'd come to school without lunch. She'd never say if she forgot it or if there was nothing at home to take. Mica made sure that she packed twice the amount of lunch she needed every day so Anca wouldn't be hungry.

Anca remembered the exciting stories Mica had told her about how the gift of diamonds had come into her life.

It all began when Mica's father and his brother had to escape Transylvania when the Fascists stormed into their town during World War ll:

"*When the soldiers went to sleep, my uncle Simion, my mother, and my father, who had been hiding in the church's cellar, came out and fled Spera. My mother never wanted to talk about it, but my father told me they walked by night and slept by day in the forest for weeks until they got to Bucharest. They all joined the Resistance.*"

"*And the diamonds?*" Anca had asked.

"*It was 1944, when my father and his brother were working out of an underground cellar in Bucharest. On Christmas day, uncle Simion was there, alone. He made all the false passports and documents—he was their expert. A man dressed in a fur coat knocked on the door and said, 'Pax-tibi.' That was the password. Peace to you. My uncle opened the door.*"

"*'I need two passports immediately,' the man told my uncle. 'For myself and my wife.'*"

"*Simion said nothing, but he let the man in and then locked the door. 'My wife is pregnant. I don't want her to give birth in this country.'*"

"*The man pleaded with Simion. 'Raoul Wallenberg in Budapest is arranging protective passes for Hungarian Jews—documents that say the holder is a Swedish citizen. I am Jewish. I speak Hungarian. You must help me get to him.'*"

"*Before my uncle could answer, the man took off his coat and opened a small, leather sack that was hidden in the fur lining.*"

"*'I'm a jeweler. I have a fabulous treasure.'*"

"Diamonds rolled on Simion's desk. They were red, green, yellow, white, and blue.

"'You can have all these diamonds,' the jeweler said. 'No one will ever know. I'll also give you five thousand American dollars to arrange our departure.'

"In one week, Simion, now the owner of the diamonds, prepared documents and visas to Sweden, two for the jeweler and one for himself. Because of his contacts with the Resistance in Bucharest and Budapest, and the jeweler's American dollars, Simion was able to arrange plane tickets for three passengers to Stockholm and then on to New York.

"The hardest part was leaving Romania. Simion hollowed out the heels and soles of his oldest shoes and hid twenty white diamonds there. He hid the colored diamonds in an oversized pocket watch and its leather strap. The largest diamonds, the green, red, and blue, he secreted inside the handle of a walking stick. He was so nervous he'd be caught that he gave my father the pocket watch with its strap and the walking stick. At the airport they searched Simion from top to bottom, but didn't inspect his shoes. They never found his white diamonds. My father, who was waiting outside the airport, went safely home with the colored diamonds.

"These diamonds helped me escape."

Marina and Cristina had not escaped as Mica and Anca had. They were what Ceausescu had labeled German-Romanians, ethnics who had a German heritage and spoke German at home. Ceausescu realized he could make money by "selling" them, as he had before with the Jews. The truth was that German-Romanians were well received in Germany, as a means to build up the country after World War ll.

Mica and her lawyers negotiated and paid for her friends' freedom. Once they were in West Germany, both Marina and Cristina wanted to move to other countries. Mica helped Marina with the proper visas to get to the United States and Cristina to France.

Marina, determined to make a fortune in business, went immediately to New York City. Mica lent her the capital she needed to get started, and Marina leased a studio in the West Village where she arranged her kitchen as a lab and began analyzing the chemical compositions of facial creams from Romania, Hungary, Yugoslavia, and Bulgaria.

She separated the component parts of creams she had taken from the Gypsies and mixed them with herbs she bought in Spanish Harlem. She added a dab of collagen to retin-A, mixed bee pollen with vitamin E, pulverized shark cartilage with a touch of honey, and created a rejuvenating, regenerating, wrinkle-free, uniquely Romanian facial cream.

She packaged it as something regal, advertised it as foolproof, and marketed it as "secret." She guaranteed romance and sold it for a fortune. Everyone swore that her cream worked. Women looked younger, felt better, and loved longer. Men indulged, too. They felt stronger and loved better. Marina Frigidescu got richer and richer.

She moved from her studio to a penthouse on Fifth Avenue. Enjoying being rich, she bought seventeenth-century carpets, eighteenth-century furniture, nineteenth-century paintings, and twentieth-century investments.

Marina was a big woman—six feet tall. Everything about her was over-sized. Her breasts were voluptuous, as was her lifestyle. She loved to give big parties with lots of caviar and champagne. She wore oversized jewelry and dressed in exotic furs. Above all, she had an enormous heart. Everyone who knew her loved her. In all her social activities, she was the center of Romanian society in New York, the queen bee.

"*Bonjour,*" shouted Marina to Anca as they greeted each other at the front door. "*Ce mai faci, draga.* Come in. Come in," said the hostess. "Your skin looks wonderful," and she kissed Anca several times on each pink cheek.

"Marina, draga," laughed Anca and kissed her friend's ageless cheeks. Marina amused her; she was like an overgrown child who couldn't stop playing with life.

Anca entered the marbled hall, gilded with candelabras reflecting on walls lined with Venetian mirrors. She took off her coat and handed it to a butler. Looking around the apartment at all her Romanian friends chatting around Gypsy violinists, she forgot for a moment that she was in New York City.

She walked into the living room and her friends waved to her one by one. There was Sergiu, the conductor, Angela, the opera singer, Georgi, the surrealist painter, and her dear friend, Mica.

Anca greeted Mica with two kisses on her cheeks. "I'm sorry I'm late—telephone call from Cristina. She and Eugen are getting married. Did you know?"

Mica smiled. "I thought so. I saw them in Europe last week."

Mica didn't say where she saw them. Instead, apparently, to avoid any questions, she put her arm around Anca and quickly walked her away from the other guests. "I've missed you. I haven't seen you in three weeks."

"I know." Anca squeezed her friend's hand.

"André said he saw you Friday at grand rounds." Mica's husband, André, and Anca were colleagues at New York Hospital. He had helped her find a position there.

"Yes, we had a joint pediatric-cardiology case."

"He told me." Mica paused. "I had a few days off last week between rehearsals." She was a choreographer for the Martha Graham troupe. "I went to Europe for a reason. I want to tell you why."

Before she could begin, she was interrupted by a man they both knew.

"Mica Mihailescu, Anca Rr-rodescu," came the familiar voice with

its rolling Romanian r's. The short, squarely built man kissed them both. His red silk scarf got in the way, and they all laughed as he pushed it to one side, only to have it return again into his face.

"My two beauties," laughed Alec. "What a lucky man I am to be with such unusual women. Mica, forgive me for interrupting. I'm in a rush, and I want to speak to Anca privately."

"Of course." Mica had just ten minutes with Alec alone.

"I'll call you tomorrow," Mica whispered to Anca. "I need to tell you something important."

"Fine. Send my love to André and the twins," and Anca kissed her friend goodbye.

"You'll see them next weekend at the fencing tournament," Mica reminded her.

"Oh, yes. I forgot."

"I'll save you a place in the cheering squad," Mica said, as she moved through the crowd.

"Alec, I'm so happy to see you." Anca smiled and gave her full attention to the man who had been her friend since childhood. She recalled how her father had chosen Alec, his brightest student at the university, to work secretly with him on radio transmissions. Sundays in their hidden basement, Alec and her father had deciphered secret codes for the anti-communist partisans.

"I haven't seen you in weeks," Anca said. "I thought you were too busy for Sunday pleasures."

"Perhaps," he said, "but I came because I knew you and Mica would be here. I had to speak to you both."

Alec Hirsch had dedicated his life to helping Romanian artists make a new life in the United States. He took them into his home, fed them, and advised them. He briefed them on business matters and introduced them to the right managers and agents. No successful Romanian artist started in the United States without first consulting Alec.

"Anca," he said, as he took her arm to walk her into another room. "One of my writer friends told me you're not limiting your life to medicine."

She laughed. "Can anything happen in New York without your knowing? Admit that you work for the CIA."

He didn't answer. Instead he took her face in his hands. *"Draga,* you're all my children. I must take care of you all." He waved his arm at the room of guests as if he were blessing them. "Especially you. I promised your father to *always* watch over you."

She took his arm. "Alec, you can help me."

Anca trusted him. She had put her life in his hands many years ago when she escaped from Romania in one of his tractors. After that, Alec had been her protector in New York.

"Something is not right. I'm being harassed. Maybe Sandra is, too. Is it possible the Romanian secret police are pursuing us?"

"Yes," he said earnestly, his entire body seemed charged with anger. "There's something very important going on right now in Romania and your words are too incendiary. No one should get curious about Romania—not now."

"What are you talking about?"

"Stop now. You're a doctor, not a political activist. You're talking on the radio about classified information without even realizing it's classified. In one of your recent messages, you spoke about a medical supply company in Transylvania. Without realizing it, you stumbled on something highly secretive. You have given the Romanian authorities a tip that something is brewing. You're talking too much. You'll put yourself, Sandra, and Petre into real danger."

A waiter passed by with champagne. Anca angrily grabbed a glass. She was annoyed that Alec was telling her what to do. Above all, she was concerned for her daughter. She'd have to phone

Sandi and take a stronger stand with her about her rebellious attitude.

Alec stared at Anca as she very quickly finished her drink. "I'm thirsty," she said, glaring at him. Then she abruptly changed her tone to a more conciliatory one. "Is something going to happen that I should know about? Why do you mention Petre now?"

"I have sources that verify what you're researching for the *Times,* is true—but truth is the last thing we want."

She stared at him. Who was *we*? How did he know what she was researching? Alec was at the center of foreign investments between Romania and America, but exactly what he did, she had never quite figured out. Painting and art, she suspected, were cover-ups for more colorful interests.

He finished his drink. "Let's meet tomorrow evening for dinner. There's a lot we should discuss, privately. First, you must assure me that you will stop broadcasting and meeting with the *Times.*"

Anca didn't answer him, but she felt a tear stream down her face. She knew she had stumbled into something dangerous. Alec wiped her tears with his silk scarf. "Don't worry," he said and took her in his burly arms. "I have friends in Washington. I'll get you and Sandra protection."

She leaned against his chest and for a second, felt relieved.

"Anca…" Alec wasn't finished talking to her. He took her hand and looked her in the eyes. "It seems your research for the *Times* has mixed your medical knowledge with political implications."

"Medicine and politics? Not intentionally."

He came closer to her and said, "You were correct when you found out that the American government has come upon a secret institute in Transylvania that's registered as a medical supply company. What you don't know is that the medical company is a cover-up. Their license says they manufacture fuel rods for use in kidney diseases."

"Fuel rods for kidney diseases. That's true—it's done."

Alec continued. "Let me take your research one step further. When special, high speed centrifuges and reactors enrich uranium oxide to a much higher level, they convert uranium into radioactive fuel rods that can be used also for nuclear weapons, not just medical equipment."

Then he looked around. People were watching them. He hesitated, and then said, "We can discuss this more tomorrow evening. Let's go outside on the terrace for now. I want to smoke."

She knew Alec trusted very few people.

Outside, he lit a cigarette. "Ceausescu has been a middleman for Gaddafi and Arafat for twenty years. The seeds of terrorism can be found in these three men. They are the ones responsible for modern-day terrorism, beginning with converting uranium secretly into nuclear weapons in Romania."

Anca sat down and took a deep breath.

"Foreign policy takes years of planning," Alec said. "These three men have come together with a common goal and have also combined their personal ambitions: Ceausescu wants to be rich, Gaddafi wants to be the leader of the Arab world, and Arafat is obsessed by the idea of ruling a Jerusalem devoid of Jews.

"We are entering into a time with a different type of warfare, as you know. It's highly effective and less expensive than ever before. The terrorists will use people as human bombs, in different ways, strapping explosives to their bodies and driving explosive-laden vehicles to blow up buildings and people. Their goal is to break up our peaceful societies, causing terror and fear from within, and from outside as well."

"Sounds like a reign of terror."

"Yes, and it's starting in Romania with the development of nuclear weapons. Ceausescu started with Gaddafi. 'We should be exporting arms and weapons,' Ceausescu told him. 'Any way and every way.' They teamed up, created a joint program of chemical and bacteriological weapons. The code name was *Brutus* from brucellosis. That business venture earned Ceausescu $350 million in cash.

"Greedy, Ceausescu wanted more money from Gaddafi. So, he set up a military camp in Transylvania to train Libyans and Palestinians to be suicide bombers. Arafat got involved and supplied the soldiers, or should I say the *human bombs.* Ceausescu wanted to be the first in everything he did, and he was. He was the first to set up terrorist training camps and to send killers to Western Europe to blow up trains and schools and...."

Anca put her arm around Alec. He was sweating despite the cold. "How do you know all this?" she asked. "This must be classified information. What does this have to do with me? I just did some research about a secret medical supply company and suggested that someone, other than the Romanian authorities, should find out what that means."

"Let's go inside. I'll continue tomorrow," he said. "There's more."

As they left the terrace, Anca was deep in thought. Alec's words had upset her, and she decided to change the conversation to another subject. "You said something before about Petre. Do you ever see him? Does he ask about me?"

"Yes."

"I can't be free of him," she confessed. "I've tried, but I can't. It's as if he's always with me. I look at Sandra and I see him. I look in this room filled with Romanians, and I feel his presence. I've tried so hard over the years to love again. I want to believe he wronged me, and not forgive him, but I can't. It's been so long and he's still inside me."

"Petre has a strength that I've never seen before. He has a mission; perhaps that's why he's so courageous."

"Selfish, too." She looked down and closed her eyes. "I remember reading Pascal years ago," she said. "I was struck by his thought: *Le cœur a ses raisons que la raison ne connaît point*—the heart has reasons that reason can never know."

"Maybe you're right not to give him up. Trust your instincts."

"I didn't know you were a romantic," she teased, as she thought again of Pascal's words on love.

"*Ma chère,*" he said as his eyes filled with light, "I admire Petre. Very few men can change history." He took her hand. "Remember you were once Petre's wife. You share a daughter whom you both adore. People know that. You should stay quiet so as not to bring attention to yourself or to him."

Realizing that he was saying more than he had intended, he stopped. "It's late." Looking at his watch he commented in a businesslike tone, "I have an appointment."

Anca smiled. "You're a dear."

Alec kissed her goodbye and whispered, "Dinner at eight. I'll call you with the address."

He left without stopping to talk to the several men and women who were vying for his attention. Anca moved into an empty room to reflect on Alec's revelations.

9

BUCHAREST, ROMANIA

> *The melancholy joys of evils passed, for he who much has suffered, much will know.*

— HOMER, THE ODYSSEY, BOOK 15

THE BRANCHES of snow-burdened trees hung heavily despite the wind. No one was walking outside; no children were playing. It was a bitter Sunday afternoon in Bucharest, a time of discontent. Petre approached the train station and studied the schedule. A wait of ten minutes. He entered the shabby hut marked *BILETE*, tickets.

"One way?" asked the surprised clerk. "It's cheaper to buy a round-trip." He eyed Petre suspiciously.

"One way. I'm a doctor. I have to see a patient in Timisoara. I'm not sure how long I'll be there." He turned his head to indicate he didn't want to talk further.

"Whatever you say." The clerk's coarse hand ripped the ticket from the pad. He had been trained not to ask questions. "Next."

Petre looked around the unlit room to make sure no one had followed him, and then he searched for a place to sit. There were no chairs, no benches. The best he could hope for was a segment of the wall to lean against. He took off his hat and walked over to an empty space to be alone. He pressed his back against a poster of the Ceausescus, his rear covering their mouths. He took a newspaper from his coat pocket and pretended to read it.

In his mind, he was reviewing the layout of Timisoara, the city where freedom would begin for his country. He calculated how many rifles, machine guns, and cannons he and his men had stored in the church's vestry. He started deciding which men would ride the fifteen tanks that his colleagues had recently purchased in Vienna and Nice. The tanks had been transported overland, inside covered vans, one at a time, during the day, taking different country routes to avoid suspicion. At night, they were hidden inside garages in multiple farms and abandoned factories, spread out in a radius of twenty kilometers from Timisoara, until needed.

Petre turned the pages of his newspaper while tallying how much money had been wired for arms, wondering if they had bought enough sniper rifles. He kept thinking, plotting, and scheming about what he and his group had been planning for twenty years. Every step had been reviewed and discussed, over and over again, in Vienna, Budapest, Paris, Nice, Moscow, New York, and Washington.

He unbuttoned his coat, growing warmer with excitement. His plans would soon be executed. At the sound of the train's whistle, he put the newspaper back in his pocket. Before he reached the platform, he saw an unusually large number of soldiers. There were dozens of them, lining up to get into the train. Each one carried a semiautomatic rifle and wore three belts of bullets.

Petre hesitated as the boarding began. Should he delay his trip to warn his men of the possibility that Ceausescu's army had been informed? There was no more time. A soldier poked him with a rifle. "Move in."

He had no choice. If he didn't enter, the soldier would become suspicious, question him, and ask to see his identity papers. Petre climbed the five steps into the train, despite his increased concern.

Walking into a car, he spied a priest in a black robe sitting alone in a private compartment, reading a book. Moving cautiously toward the door, Petre sat down in a vacant seat opposite the man and eyed the long scar under his right eye. Reverend Sandor Mokess, his deputy in Timisoara, had told Petre that this priest would be his contact man.

"Good morning. *Buna dimineata,*" said the priest, still pretending to read.

"The fire is burning from east to west," said Petre.

The priest registered the code and answered accordingly. "Yes, a friend will come to direct the flames."

"I'm that friend." Petre settled into his seat and casually commented, "At least seven hours to Timisoara."

"*Da,*" the priest answered respectfully. "We'll have to change trains."

Petre responded. "I'm going to Timisoara to see the Reverend. He needs a doctor." Those were the final words to indicate they recognized each other.

The priest picked up the conversation with small talk. "A lot of Hungarians live there. About three hundred miles from the Hungarian border in the Banat region—near Serbia—accessible to Transylvania."

Petre didn't say anything; just stared at the man for several seconds. The priest, appearing slightly uncomfortable with the silence, looked down. Petre continued to study him. Thin, but with broad shoulders and strongly built, the man looked more like a worker than a priest. Petre noticed his hands were square, coarse, red, and cut at the knuckles. Reverend Mokess had told Petre that he had chosen this priest to contact other revolutionary priests from Greek Orthodox and Lutheran churches.

"I brought my doctor's bag and antibiotics," Petre said. "Think I'll need them?"

"Yes." The priest pointed his finger at dozens of soldiers on the platform.

"Why so many?" Petre inquired, trying to sound nonchalant. He needed to probe to see if the priest was an informer and to see if he had reported Petre's presence.

"It's not what you think. They're going to the Hungarian border because the famous athlete, Nimech, has disappeared. She hid herself for two days in the trunk of a friend's car in Transylvania. Then, she and her friend escaped in the middle of the night. Ceausescu's son, Nicu, is in love with her. He has the police searching to bring her back."

Petre nodded. He remembered seeing her at a party at the presidential palace. Nicu had been drunk.

"Are you ill?" Petre asked the priest, who was opening the window.

"I'm fine. I just need a minute of fresh air and then I'll close it."

Petre understood the constant surveillance, the need to check on anyone and anything suspicious. He also looked out the window to study the soldiers surrounding the train. Their number was increasing.

He moved closer to the priest. "Did you know Reverend Mokess was beaten up and stabbed last month?" Petre was testing the priest. How much did he know about Mokess?

"Yes, I visited him last week. He was hiding in the church, but he's home now. His wife is pregnant." He stopped short as a soldier barged into their compartment, pointing a machine gun at them.

"Show me your IDs," the soldier ordered. He was young, not more than sixteen years old. Ceausescu recruited orphans and raised them for his army; he thought it would guarantee loyalty.

Petre took out his official governmental ID.

"Oh." The boy's face turned pale as he stepped to attention. "Comrade Nicolae Ceausescu's private doctor."

The child soldier clicked his heels together, nodded in deference, and left the men alone. The priest straightened his black robe while looking at Petre out of the corner of his eye. Petre stood up, moved to the door of their compartment, opened it, looked down the corridor, studied the hallway, and closed the door tight. He wondered if there would be consequences. Would the soldier question why Ceausescu's doctor was traveling to Timisoara? Would he talk to the other soldiers?

The priest resumed the conversation. "You must know Ceausescu well."

"I guess you can say that. He's seventy-one years old, five foot-five tall, overweight, takes insulin every day for diabetes, and has high blood pressure. He's borderline schizophrenic and highly paranoid. Every photo of him from the press is retouched to show him taller, younger, thinner, smarter, and better. I can never forget that he believes he's greater than anyone in the world."

"Did you know he's also a thief?"

"Sure. He's stolen life from every Romanian for twenty-four years."

Then Petre asked, "Tell me, what's your name? We haven't introduced ourselves."

"Mihai Strancusi."

"Petre Ilianu."

They shook hands; their eyes met. Petre didn't have to think further about who would hand out the arms. The choice had already been made by Mokess, and Petre agreed. Mokess, the thirty-seven-year old Lutheran pastor from Timisoara, was in charge of organizing the opposition. He had told Petre that he'd entrust the guns to his most reliable man, a man of God.

One of Petre's responsibilities had been to identify and enlist several generals and politicians from Ceausescu's inner circle who opposed the dictator and were approved by both the Russians and Americans to work together. Their strategy was to channel the agitation from Timisoara to Bucharest and then get rid of the dictator.

Alec worked with the CIA in Washington. He and his group were in charge of sharing intelligence with Gorbachev and the KGB in Moscow.

Mica was working from New York with her contacts at the United Nations. For many years, as they were all planning the revolution, Mica, with her money from selling the diamonds, had created an NGO with UNICEF to aid Romanian orphans in Transylvania. Her parents, now safely in New York, had agreed that income from the diamonds should be used to help others.

Mica's U.N. work also allowed her access to well-placed Romanian diplomats and officials who were ready to switch sides. They knew the Americans were willing to pay them for their loyalty. Mica had also learned that Romania was training secret agents to work with the U.S. to identify Eastern European countries dealing in small arms. These contacts helped Mica get the best price for weapons.

Eugen and Cristina in Paris, with Marina and Mica in New York, raised the money to buy weapons and Alec coordinated the deliveries.

Petre was at the center of all their activities, coordinating with everyone. His assignment was to begin the revolution in Timisoara.

Petre took off his coat. Despite the unheated train, he wanted to feel at ease. He resumed his conversation with his companion with the intention to create a personal bond. "The Romanian government has always had a good army. The best in Eastern Europe since World War ll."

"Well, they learned a lot from the Nazis." The priest's mouth tightened.

Petre lowered his eyes. "They've taught a lot to the P.L.O. The Romanian army has been secretly training P.L.O. pilots in the Carpathian Mountains for years. I overheard Ceausescu talking on the phone about this to his ministers."

The priest moved closer to Petre. "Terrorists. Follow their money trail and you'll smell their odor. Ceausescu would do anything for money. Look what he did in Afghanistan. He got plenty of cash to train the Mujahideen for the Americans who knew a Russian defeat in Afghanistan would be the beginning of a Soviet decline with a domino effect."

Petre interrupted him. "Then Gorbachev realized that Ceausescu, who helped bring down Russia in Afghanistan, could bring him down as well."

The priest moved closer to Petre. "There's one thing that puzzles me. Why did Gorbachev and Ceausescu have a falling out?"

Petre snapped his fingers as if the answer was easy. "Gorbachev wanted *perestroika,* so that he could introduce private enterprise. Ten years in Afghanistan had weakened the Soviet economy."

"I see," the priest said. "I imagine Ceausescu wanted communism to continue so he could stay in power. Continue his business deals with his corrupt friends."

"Yes. Economics precedes politics," Petre commented.

The priest nodded. "There's one important piece of the riddle you didn't mention about Afghanistan. Who was Ceausescu's contact man?"

Petre smiled. "It was Arafat. He sold the arms to Romania. Then, Ceausescu sold them to the Afghan Mujahideen and trained them. The armaments' markings were altered so that they couldn't be traced back to Romania or the PLO."

For several seconds there was an uncomfortable silence. Petre decided to talk of something else. "Did you know that the Shah of Iran and the Ayatollah both called Ceausescu a *good communist partner?* Because of his *goodness,* he got millions of dollars from both Iranian leaders. Then Ceausescu transferred the cash to gold."

The priest stared at Petre and then blessed him.

He probably thinks I have the devil in me, Petre thought. *Why am I talking so much? Not like me. Am I making my last confession to this priest before the end? Am I showing my nervousness?*

Petre changed the subject again and said firmly, "Let's talk about our next steps in Timisoara. I need you to arrange with the Serbian priest to rally all the Serbs living in the area. It's in their interest to be with us. Also, contact the leaders of the miners, the students, the factory workers. Tell them all to come to Mokess's house tonight at nine o'clock for a meeting. I have orders for you to pass on to all the revolutionaries. Tell them they should not try to be independent. Dissent will weaken the revolution. We share a common goal: to take away the sufferings of the people and give them freedom."

The priest moved uncomfortably in his seat. "Please forgive me for prying. I'm just a clergyman, but can I ask you how you got to this point of planning the uprising?" He paused respectfully and waited.

"It's a *revolution,*" Petre corrected him. Then he softened his tone. "I was working in a small town in the region of Transylvania from 1967 to 1970. A typhus epidemic broke out there. I got medicine from friends and gave it to the peasants."

"Medicine?" he asked. The priest realized that Petre had broken the law. He remembered himself how he had been imprisoned for opening a church and exposing the statue of the Crying Saint so the people could pray.

Petre opened the window and pretended to study the land-
scape. In reality, whenever he wanted to prevent a personal
connection, he retreated into himself and stopped any further
conversation. He'd concentrate on something private to distance
himself even more. Often, he'd think of Anca.

He tried to conjure up the image of her that first day when they
met in front of the clinic. She had slipped in the mud because she
was staring at him and had missed the steps.

Petre closed his eyes, but he lost her image. He lost her warmth
to his dreams for revolution and freedom.

"You must have had very important friends who helped you.
Medicine?" The priest couldn't refrain from repeating.

Petre didn't answer. His thoughts turned to what he had to do
in the days to come. When he finally did speak, he said, "In 1965
when Ceausescu came to power, I was twenty-one. My father was
the leader of the anti-communists. He was killed."

Petre paused. He couldn't forget that his father had died in his
arms. The communists had a secret system of getting rid of their
opponents. They'd irradiate their offices or houses, and the victim
would die from radioactive exposure.

He remembered the tragic moment when his father died, and
when his own commitment to end tyranny had fomented in his
heart.

---

*It was the summer of 1965. Petre was in Cluj to join his father at an anti-
communist rally.*

*"Prieteni, friends, listen to me," Petre yelled into a bullhorn. "Haven't
you had enough of communism? Let's all unite and finish this evil!"*

There were cheers and hoorays from the crowd.

"Move on! Move on!" the police roared.

"Go home!" the soldiers warned.

The crowd threw rocks. Students set fire to the town hall and the police sprayed them with water hoses.

Moments later, there was pandemonium and Petre saw his father, the leader of the uprising, fall to the ground. Petre ran to him, picked him up in his arms.

"Tata, Father." Tears streamed down Petre's face as he stroked his father's hair.

Then the white head dropped. Petre rocked his father as if he were putting him to sleep. A wagon stopped in front of them. A man, crying, took the body and put it into the wagon. "He was given a Radu."

Petre knew what that meant—a code word for radiating the enemy.

"I was a swimmer then," he told the priest, "a member of Romania's national team. The communists took me despite my background because they needed me to win. When we had a competition in Vienna, I was the first to race, and I won. That night, when everyone was sleeping, I escaped by walking all night to a village in the countryside. I hid in an abandoned factory with a backpack filled with food."

Petre abruptly stopped talking. He stood up to pace the compartment. He retreated into his inner world and remembered that when his father had died, he had an opportunity to escape. It was in 1965 when he had just finished medical school and was Romania's champion swimmer. His father's friends, who were working for the U.S. government in Vienna, had a plan for him to defect and to study endocrinology for two years in the States.

He had been a Fellow at Johns Hopkins when he heard that Ceausescu was visiting President Lyndon Johnson. Petre went to Washington, D.C. with the hope of hearing Ceausescu give a speech before the Senate. Arriving early, he saw Ceausescu outside the Capitol Building being interviewed by several American journalists.

As Ceausescu was talking, he faltered and then fainted. A dozen bodyguards, Romanian as well as American, rushed over to him. Petre did, too. He spoke Romanian to Ceausescu's guards, and they told him the dictator was diabetic. Petre explained the problem to the American Secret Service: Ceausescu had taken too much insulin that day, thinking the American syringe was the same size as the Romanian one. The overdose had caused his blood sugar to drop quickly, making him faint.

The Americans rushed Ceausescu to Johns Hopkins Hospital. Several days later, the dictator's wife, Elena, saw Petre during rounds. Elena had been trained as a chemist and was eager to speak with him. Impressed with how quickly Petre had realized Ceausescu's problem, and equally impressed that he was attractive and unmarried, she asked him if he would return to Romania with them and serve as their personal doctor. Petre took advantage of the fortuity of events; he was already planning revenge for his father's death.

At that moment, Petre realized that fate had tapped him. Destiny had given him an opportunity to play actor and killer. He'd be able to hide behind a disguise of being the personal doctor to a tyrant and keeping him alive, until the right moment came to slaughter him for his crimes.

The young doctor left the US to prepare. He returned to Romania in 1967.

After working for several months for the Ceausescu family, news spread throughout the country about a typhus epidemic in Transylvania. Chance, again, had played into Petre's hands. He took a leave of absence as Ceausescu's doctor, which the dictator reluctantly allowed.

Petre had a secret weapon: medicine—tetracycline, antibiotics, and vaccines. No one knew they came from his contacts in America. It was part of a plan for Petre to make inroads and friends in Transylvania and begin his clandestine work.

Not all things can be planned or calculated, especially those of the heart. During that time, Petre and Anca worked together in the clinic, fell in love, and married; but when Anca got pregnant, Ceausescu was still in power. Petre hadn't yet achieved his goal. He wasn't ready to leave the country. To send Anca and the baby to a safer place was part of his plans. As for joining them with another defective tractor, that was something he would not do. He truly believed the revolution wouldn't take so long and that he'd join his family in the States.

Events, however, did not move as quickly as Petre wanted. It took many years for the Russians to loosen their control over Romania and for the Russians to agree with the Americans on a mutual, beneficial strategy to dismantle communism, despite the Cold War.

Soon after Anca escaped, Nicu Ceausescu contacted typhus. Petre was summoned by the dictator to return to Bucharest. He nursed the son with his medicines, medicines that couldn't be found anywhere in Romania, not even for a dictator. The parents never questioned what type of treatment Nicu was given; they just wanted him cured. When Nicu was well, his mother was so grateful that she offered Petre one of her diamond bracelets as a gift.

"No," Petre said. "I don't know anyone who could wear it, and it doesn't fit me."

Elena Ceausescu laughed. "Petre, you're a charming man and very handsome. You should stay in Bucharest, nearer to me." She winked at him and took his hand. "What beautiful fingers you have. Sensitive. I imagine they must feel soft on skin." She moved closer to him.

He shifted slightly away. "Helps me percuss better a patient's chest, to find out how large the heart is."

"Maybe in Bucharest you can show me how you do that. I have a big heart."

"That's a doctor's secret," and he smiled.

"Don't return to that muddy town in Transylvania," she said. "I'm the president of the Academy of Sciences and Medicine. I can give you permission to publish articles and present them at international meetings. You'll be able to travel."

He pretended to hesitate while she tried to convince him. "I know your father was an anti-communist and that you defected to America. No one else knows this. I can rip up those papers that are in your file."

Could he trust her? No other Romanian doctor had been trained in endocrinology in the States and then returned to Romania. No doctor in the country had access to the life-saving medicines he had.

Petre thought of Rasputin and how he had worked closely with the Czarina of Russia to rule the Russian Empire. She had believed Rasputin was keeping her son, Alexis, alive just like Elena seemed to believe that Petre was keeping her husband alive. Petre thought of his own motives and of his valuable contacts with the Americans.

Petre raised his finger to make the sign of the cross and said to Elena, smilingly, "God has willed it. I agree."

The priest moved uncomfortably in his seat. Petre had suddenly stopped talking and seemed to be deep in his own thoughts. The priest was probably afraid he had angered him by asking too many questions. Petre was simply in the grip of his memories.

The most invigorating time of his life was when he was in Baltimore. Mornings were spent in the clinic at Johns Hopkins Hospital seeing patients. In the afternoons, he'd drive to McLean,

Virginia where he trained secretly at CIA headquarters as a covert operative. His father's colleagues had arranged the details.

There were three men in Petre's group—Egyptian, Jordanian, and Romanian. Rarely did they train together or even see each other. Petre worked alone with one CIA officer who said his name was John. They worked for months to perfect Petre's knowledge of explosives, firearms, ground vehicles, and military tanks, so he'd be able to match the talents of each member of his group to the needed skill.

It was the training in hand-to-hand combat that Petre enjoyed the most. It reminded him of wrestling, a test of one's courage to meet the enemy face to face. Petre had been gifted with quick reflexes, good timing, and balance. He was also an excellent shot. It was a time of his life when he was challenged physically and intellectually—a time to prepare to return to his country with American medicines and CIA friends. It was a time to lead a coup d'état.

That was the good side of his past. There was the other face, the face of shame, when he had hurt the person he loved the most —Anca. As he thought of her, his guilt increased. He hated himself for deceiving her, for making her life more difficult. He was ashamed of what he had done.

He had tried over the years to free himself from her with the help of a pretty face or a one-night stand. No matter how many years had passed, he was never able to stop loving her, or to keep thinking about her.

Anca's face always returned. He remembered how he enjoyed kissing her swollen stomach and talking to the little person inside. "I hope you're a girl and you'll look like your mother."

Anca had laughed. "I hope the baby looks like you, so I will always have you."

Petre moved toward the window in the train and closed his eyes against the icy pane.

10

NEW YORK CITY

ANCA WALKED over to the bar in Marina's opulent dining room. She kept thinking about what Alec had just told her, and how frightening it was.

She asked the bartender for a glass of scotch. Trying to distract herself, she focused on Marina talking to a group of men. They were apparently mesmerized by a story she was telling about how she had started her career. Directly from the Lyceum in Spera, Marina had gone to work at the geriatric clinic, the Parhon Institute, in Bucharest with Dr. Ana Aslan who was experimenting with *Gerovital H3,* an anti-aging treatment.

Dr. Aslan believed that daily injections of procaine and benzoic acid could slow down the aging process. She even used special injections for sexual rejuvenation for men as well as for women. She became so popular that her institute gained a reputation as a mecca for the international jet set. Taking her treatments were VIP's like Charles De Gaulle, Mao Zedong, Ho Chi Minh, Nikita Khrushev, the Ceausescus, and even President John Kennedy. They all needed to stay strong.

Anca sipped her drink and smiled as she watched Marina in the middle of her admirers.

Once settled in Manhattan, Marina mixed her ingredients in her kitchen-laboratory, and then opened a salon for facial creams on Madison Avenue and 53rd Street, next to St. Patrick's Rectory. Mica had become her financial backer. They had faith the address would bring good luck—and it did.

Marina's strategy was to teach women that their skin was an asset. "Use your beauty for power" was Marina's motto. The words were displayed in gold letters in her salon's waiting room, encouraging women to be confident.

As Anca drifted away from Marina and the group of people surrounding her, a tall, full-faced woman with Asiatic eyes, high cheekbones, full lips, and alabaster skin approached her. Anca thought she could have been a model for one of Brancusi's marble sculptures.

"*Anca Rodescu!* It's so good to see you," she said.

"Oh, Livia. What are you doing here?" Anca said as she kissed the smooth, white cheek.

Livia was a Romanian friend of Cristina's; both of them had studied fashion design in Paris.

"Are you still working at the Louvre?" Anca asked.

"Yes, but I'm in New York for a few weeks, putting together a show of peasant dresses from Eastern Europe for the Metropolitan Museum."

Two men in their mid-sixties, both with white hair, came over to the women.

"*Livia,*" said the shorter man, and kissed her hand Romanian style.

"Florin, Nicky. I didn't realize you knew Marina."

"Doesn't everyone?" answered the taller one.

Livia kissed him hello. "Florin, this is Dr. Anca Rodescu, from your part of Transylvania."

They all greeted each other.

"Anca," continued Livia in a loud voice, as if the men were deaf, "Florin and Nicky know Cristina." Then turning to the men she said, "Anca and Cristina are best friends."

"Oh," smiled Florin. "We know Cristina from a couple of business deals. In fact, we helped her out last week with a transaction in Nice. She was with her fiancé and another lady, named Mica."

Anca wondered what exactly her friends were doing in Nice. Cristina had said on the phone that she had been there for a business investment, but she didn't elaborate on the details. Why was Mica with her?

"Florin and Nicky are textile manufacturers," Livia told Anca. "They're the businessmen behind Paris's fashion world. My investors. Cristina's too."

"Which town are you from?" Anca asked, smiling warmly.

"Cluj. A long time ago."

"I studied medicine there, although I was born in a smaller town in Transylvania."

"Ah, Cluj. What a coincidence. You're a doctor?"

"Yes, a pediatrician."

Livia, seeing some friends in the room, kissed the men goodbye and left Anca in their company.

Florin moved closer to Anca. He trusted her since she was part of Cristina's and Marina's circle of friends. "There's trouble in Timisoara and Transylvania."

"How do you know?"

"We have workers there. The women who sew for us said all the men in the region have left their towns to go to Timisoara."

"Why Timisoara?"

"It's far from Bucharest, less supervision, and less press. Lots of ethnic-Hungarians live there. They're good fighters. The priest there is a leader—an honest man." He glanced around, then lowered his voice. "They say a revolution is smoldering."

"The Romanian-Hungarians living in Timisoara are starting it," added Nicky.

"The Russians and Americans want Ceausescu out. A revolution is the best way."

There were too many coincidences, thought Anca: Evdochia phoning her from Romania; Marina using her party as a meeting ground; Mica and Cristina together recently in Nice; Alec in contact with Petre; and she being harassed. Anca tried to put the pieces together.

"I need to speak to someone in the other room," she said. "I'm sorry." She needed to be alone.

"Anca, Anca!" came a voice from a neighboring group.

She spied Georgi, an artist. She wondered why Marina had invited him. Was he part of the puzzle?

Anca tried to avoid him by pretending she hadn't heard her name. He shouted to her again from across the room. A waiter turned to her and pointed to Georgi. "Someone is trying to get your attention."

Georgi approached her. He was a modernist painter of some renown. She didn't like his art, or him. He had started his career in Berlin, stealing ideas from unknown artists exhibiting in small galleries and then marketing their ideas in New York as his own.

Word had spread among the Romanian community that Georgi had not cooperated with investigators about the biggest painting heist in decades. A Van Gogh, a Matisse, a Picasso, and four old masters had been stolen from a museum in Rotterdam. Georgi told authorities that he knew the twenty-nine-year-old thief who came from the same town as he did, near the Romanian-Yugoslavian border. When Georgi was interrogated, he kept changing his story. One day, he said he thought the thief's mother had burned the paintings in her furnace. The next time, he said she had buried them in a cemetery. Or had they been sold to an emir in Qatar—or was it a Kuwaiti prince?

"I hear Cristina is getting married," he said.

Cristina and Georgi had been colleagues together at the Art Institute in Bucharest. Before their final exam in design, Georgi had borrowed Cristina's art books to study. He never returned them; he told Cristina he had lost them. Georgi got such a high grade that he won a scholarship to study art in Berlin. Then he defected to the States.

"Who's the lucky guy?"

"Eugen Simionescu. Do you know him?"

"Eugen?" he said, surprised, almost dropping his drink. "When I was imprisoned in East Berlin for giving an avant-garde exhibit, Eugen was the one who got me out. Eugen has a lot of contacts."

Anca glanced around to see who was watching them talk.

Georgi continued in a low voice. "I've heard rumors that Gorbachev is working with the Americans and Brits. You know —*perestroika, glasnost.* I've also heard that Gorbachev won't protect Ceausescu anymore. I don't discount a revolution in Romania. They'll use a solid citizen, someone anti-communist so the people will follow him. Then they'll get rid of him and put in their own man. Not the first time that's happened," he concluded cynically. "Today's hero, tomorrow's victim."

Anca leaned against the wall. The pieces were coming together: a revolution in Timisoara; a training camp for Arabs in the Carpathian Mountains; an institute of nuclear weapons in Transylvania.

Oh, my God, she thought, *is Petre in Timisoara or Transylvania? Is that why he told Sandra he can't meet her for Christmas vacation?*

"What's the matter?" asked Georgi. "Are you okay? You look pale."

"I have to do something," she said, and left him standing there.

As she passed the fireplace, she stopped for a minute to lean against the wall. She was dizzy. She wondered if she was getting sick. She remembered how ill she had been years ago.

"Anca, you're not being careful enough," Petre had reprimanded her. "Open your mouth," he said. "Stick out your tongue."

"Maybe I'm tired because I'm pregnant," she laughed, teasing him.

"I told you not to go into their lice-infected huts." Seeing red blisters in her mouth and spots of pus inside her throat, he snapped at her. "You never listen to me!"

"I don't have typhus," she said defiantly.

"You waited too long to vaccinate yourself."

"I won't let myself get sick."

"You think your willpower can suppress disease? Get into bed this minute. I'm closing the clinic to take care of you. One patient is enough for me."

For ten days he didn't leave her side. Morning, noon and night, he spoon-fed her juices and fruit and sponge-bathed her with alcohol to keep the fever down. He didn't leave her for a minute, always checking that she had enough medicine, blankets, and water.

One afternoon, he had fallen asleep in the chair, exhausted. Anca got out of bed, went over to him, caressed his hair, and kissed his neck. Waking up, he stared into her blue-green eyes and wondered if he was dreaming. She put her head on his chest and whispered, "I'm better."

He took her in his arms.

She moved closer and said tenderly, "You saved two lives."

PART II

A PLAN

MONDAY, DECEMBER 11,1989

Odysseus makes himself known to Penelope

11

NEW YORK CITY

ANCA TWISTED and turned in bed. Images of Petre prevented her from sleeping. *He was climbing up a mountain. The path was narrow and rocky. Packs of wolves howling. Smoke. Fire. At the top of the mountain was a building. A man with a rifle jumped out. "What are you doing here?"*

Anca woke up, sweating and trembling. "Thank God it wasn't real," she reasoned and then wondered why she was thinking about Petre so much. It was 7:00 a.m. and her thoughts went to rounding with her students and interns. Then she remembered she had rescheduled her day to go first to the *Times* for an editorial meeting. Alec had asked her not to work with them any longer, but she was curious to see if the meeting would reveal a reason why Alec was being so defiant with her. She decided not to cancel the appointment.

After lingering a few minutes in bed, she dialed Sandra's number.

"You've reached Sandi and Susan," announced the machine. "Speak your piece. We'll get back to you if we can."

"Sandra, this is your mother." She tried to speak calmly. "I'm home. Call me."

"Hello, hello," the voice on the other end of the line mumbled. "Don't hang up."

"Oh, Sandra. Are you all right?"

"I've been having some adventures. Nothing serious."

"Tell me." Anca didn't like her daughter's hesitant voice.

"Yesterday morning after I spoke to you, I took a walk to the gym. A guy wanted my attention." Sandra hesitated to tell her mother the full story. She had survived the crisis and thought her mother would overreact. Yet Sandra did want to know why the incident had happened. "Do you think there's a connection between the journalist and this dude?"

"Yes, and it might also have something to do with my work."

"What do you mean?"

"Some people are trying to get my attention, too."

"Yeah, but would they try to get to me to get to you?" Now Sandra sounded concerned.

"Yes. When's your last class before vacation?"

"Friday."

"I want you to come home tomorrow."

"I have two papers due on Thursday, and I have to practice with the team for the Ivies."

Sandra was stubborn, but her mother was more so. "You can mail in your papers and fence at your club in the city. We'll drive to Princeton from here. Don't tell anyone you're leaving."

"Mom, you're flipping out."

"I'll explain everything to you tomorrow. I'll be home. I'm not going to work for a few weeks."

"*What?*"

Anca always worked—seven days a week, twelve hours a day. When she returned home, she continued long into the night, reading about new developments in pediatrics, preparing lectures for her students, reviewing articles for the *Times*. Even her trips to Paris were never more than a few days. She couldn't imagine missing work.

Sandra quickly changed her tone; she knew something was wrong. "Okay, Mom, I'll take the express train that leaves New Haven at 8:00 tomorrow morning."

"Good." Anca wanted to say so much more, but simply said, "I have a plan. I'll tell you tomorrow."

Anca got out of bed, put on her blue silk bathrobe, and already full of energy, proceeded to the kitchen. When the phone rang, she felt her stomach tighten. *I hope it's not another prank call.* Then she thought of the Gypsy and decided to answer.

"Hello, Anca," said a man's deep voice.

"Mark?"

"I got in last night. I tried to call you, but you weren't home. Were you in the company of someone I should be jealous of?"

She laughed. "There's no one like you. I was at Marina's house. She gave a reception for a group of old friends."

"Oh, then I should have left a message after all."

"It's okay. Everyone was talking about politics." She didn't mention that it was all about a possible revolution in Romania. "I thought you were coming home Saturday."

"I had planned to. I even made dinner reservations for us at Aldo's, but they had me seeing more patients than I expected. Such severe cases of TB, I had to stay in L.A. They had to take advantage of having the chief from New York Hospital."

Mark reminded her of a child who swells up when he's fawned over. Despite his big ego and reputation, he was very childlike inside. She found that charming.

"I'm glad you're home. I missed you." After living with him on and off again for ten years, Anca felt lonely when he wasn't near. She was accustomed to talking with him about everything, and she knew he'd give her practical advice on how to protect Sandra.

Anca considered Mark to be her rational anchor, and he had loved Sandra as if she were his own daughter.

"Some strange things are happening," she said, walking to the window and turning her back to the walls that might be bugged. "I think my messages on Voice of America aren't popular with all my listeners."

"Anca, my love, I told you not to get involved in politics. You're a doctor, not a political activist."

She didn't dare tell him about the article she was editing for the *Times*. He had warned her a year ago not to work with them. "The wrong people will find out what you're doing," he had cautioned her.

"Something else," she said. "I have to take some time off from the hospital. I'll need coverage for the clinic and my patients." She paused as she thought about how to phrase her real question. Instead of asking outright, "Can you cover for me?" she circumvented with, "Can someone replace me?" Since becoming chairman of the department, Mark saw very few patients. She hoped he would for her.

"When do you need coverage?" he asked.

"Starting tomorrow. I'll need to be away for a few weeks."

"A few weeks? Why? Where are you going?"

She didn't answer even though he gave her a moment.

"It's Christmas time," he said. "I have to think about who can cover for you."

"Can we meet for breakfast tomorrow?"

"Breakfast? Why not dinner tonight?"

"I can't." She didn't say why not.

He sounded surprised. "Of course I'll help you. I'll look for you in the clinic this afternoon. Maybe we can chat then?"

As Anca hung up, she noticed the answering machine light blinking. There wasn't any message though. Only the clicking of repeated hang-ups. She went to her desk, took her notes for the

Times, and put several other papers into her briefcase. She picked up her omnipresent to-do list, and wrote down the address of Jonathan Curtis, editor at the *Times.*

She walked toward her closet like a soldier and selected something serious yet chic. She dressed in less time than it took her to collect her papers.

Anca couldn't find a taxi on Madison Avenue. She checked her watch. It was 9:40, and she ran toward Park Avenue, hoping to have better luck. If she caught a cab quickly, she could still be on time for her 10:00 meeting.

When she saw a taxi stop at her feet, she jumped in. "Take Park Avenue downtown. I'm in a rush."

"No," he answered and headed toward Fifth Avenue.

"Where are you going?"

"I'm crossing the park. West side better."

"Park Avenue is faster."

"Lady, I don't know what ya do, but ya don't look like ya drive a cab."

There was nothing she could do. To divert herself, she took out her papers and reviewed some notes for her meeting:

- Iran's President, Rafsanjani, since August 1989, has promised Ceausescu a number of Iranian Revolutionary Guards to protect him if there's a coup d'état in Bucharest. Why does he want to help? What does the *Times* know about Rafsanjani?
- Why is Kim Il-Sung of North Korea working with Ceausescu?

She looked up as the driver stopped at a red light on the corner of 9th Avenue and 50th Street. She moved uncomfortably in her seat, hoping not to see the building where Polyclinic Hospital used to be.

The driver passed the building and Anca remembered the first week she had arrived in New York City. She had needed to rent an apartment near the hospital.

"One bedroom? Will that do?" The landlord spit out the tip of his cigar and eyed her stomach.

"It's all I need for now." She stopped speaking as a cockroach ran across her feet.

He pretended not to notice. "I'll give you a break on the rent if you do some cleaning for the building."

Anca looked down at the cockroach. "No, I can pay the rent. I'm a doctor."

Thoughts of the past flooded her mind.

Petre had not come to her side, despite his promise. Alec had taken the defective tractor instead, and had arrived in New York at the time Anca had delivered at New York Hospital. André, Mica's husband, an Attending Physician at the hospital, had arranged the details for her delivery and care.

Her friends helped her with the baby—her surrogate family—but she suffered not having Petre near. It was Alec who had informed him that he had become the father of a beautiful baby girl. It took Anca ten years to finally communicate with Petre in a letter when she filed for a divorce.

"Ya see, lady? You'll be right there," the driver commented as he stopped at a red light. "No traffic on 9th Avenue. I was right."

Anca didn't answer. Instead, she tried to focus on her meeting. Yet her thoughts kept returning to Sandra. Until her daughter was safely home with her in New York, Anca wouldn't stop worrying.

"Dr. Rodescu," came the confident voice of Jonathan Curtis II, Editor-in-Chief of the *New York Times*. "We have engaged you, a Romanian doctor, specifically for an article about a medical supply company in Transylvania. In addition, we have followed your messages on Voice of America, which are very straight-forward, and our staff of writers have spoken highly of the research notes you prepare for them. All of this, in your favor." He paused, stared at her and continued, "We'd like to have your opinion about what details we should cover related to your country's *chaos*."

Sitting behind his antique desk, he poured himself a glass of water and tried to appear sympathetic. As he put his lips to the glass, he moved his wrist slightly at an angle and glanced at his watch. His assistant sat at a desk on the other side of the room, taking notes.

Curtis was about Anca's age, maybe a little older, somewhere in his mid-forties. He was handsome, with long blond hair that he combed straight back with some kind of fragrant gel. He was dressed in a gray striped suit, white shirt, and bright red tie. His arrogant smirk annoyed her.

"Actually, I don't think you should print anything about a medical company, not yet," she began, remembering Alec's warnings. "Let the communists think no one suspects danger." Why did Curtis use the word *chaos?* Did he know something was happening in Romania? Was he testing her?

"Okay." He shrugged. "We'll wait a few days. I'm sure we'll have a better story by then."

Anca sensed he was annoyed as he twisted his lips.

"I never could sympathize with Balkan politics," he commented. "Can't trust anyone in those countries. A lot of corruption, kickbacks, and double-crossing. Even the justice system in Romania is corrupt."

He stood up and approached the couch where she was sitting. "Another thing—it seems a large number of rifles with markings from Romania were found last week in Tunisia. Why does Gaddafi want arms now?"

Before she could speak, he answered his own question.

"Gaddafi is hiding them on the Tunisian side of the border with Libya until he needs them. He feels his demise is near."

He turned away from Anca and said to his assistant. "Put in a map tomorrow of Libya and Tunisia with an article. Something is brewing there also."

Then he returned his attention to Anca. "I've looked at your notes based on your research for us. You talk about terrorists who are guarding a nuclear institute in Transylvania. You must have *proof* for such statements."

"Yes, I believe…"

"*Believe?* We need facts. Hard evidence. We just received a letter from the Romanian government denying that they have a nuclear facility. Or, that they are 'proliferators of nuclear weapons,' as you claim."

He took another sip of water. "Above all, they deny sharing nuclear technology with rogue nations, like Libya, Iran or North Korea."

He stopped talking for a moment and picked up a paper from his desk. "Let me read to you something that you wrote for us in your notes:"

"'Kim Il-Sung was educated in Moscow during the war. After the war, in 1948, the Russians put him into power in North Korea. This was the same tactic that they used in Romania to train post-war communist leaders. The Russians also encouraged a long friendship between Romania and North Korea. Kim invited Ceausescu to Pyongyang in 1971. Then Ceausescu reciprocated and invited Kim to Bucharest in May 1975. Again, Kim invited Ceausescu to Pyongyang in May 1978.'"

"Good research," Curtis commented, "but the question is *why so many visits?* You didn't explain the reason. It was more than just a mutual admiration of their personality cult. Ceausescu sold Kim nuclear parts and technology. Yet Romania claims that they have facilities only for *researching* medical equipment. What is the truth, Dr. Rodescu?"

Anca stood up angrily and waved her own papers. "These are updated notes that indicate how Ceausescu has worked for twenty years to develop a nuclear weapons program with North Korea, Iran and Libya. Remember, Romania produces natural uranium, plutonium, and heavy water. They're essential for a nuclear program. It takes years to build up a nuclear arsenal in Romania and North Korea."

Curtis was already shaking his head.

"Interesting theory, but I need more proof. When you have *facts*, we can use your *notes* for an article. Not before. While you're gathering your facts, look into the role of Pakistan's Prime Minister, Ali Bhutto, who started to work with Ceausescu on nuclear technology and then stopped suddenly when Dr. Khan came into the picture." He took out *Time* magazine and showed her the photo. "Dr. Khan. 'Father of Pakistan's Nuclear Program.' He may become Ceausescu's competitor."

"Don't forget Ceausescu's other nuclear partners like the Shah of Iran, another business partner until Ayatollah Khomeini came back from Paris to overthrew him and became the leader of Islamic revival in Iran. And Rafsanjani—why is he such a personal friend with Ceausescu? Rafsanjani is a key figure."

Mr. Curtis showed her another *Time* magazine cover.

"You see, we have important information and *Time* magazine is giving us some facts. Maybe even *proof.*" He paused and stared hard at her. Then he filled his glass with more water. "There is something I am quite eager to print now, rather than *wait* for your notes."

"Yes?" She wasn't ready to give in to his dismissive attitude. Or to Alec's warnings.

"I'm interested in Ceausescu's friends, not only Gaddafi and Arafat—more interesting and less known, an Iranian threesome."

He walked away to the far side of the room and pointed to a wall where there were photos of leaders from around the world.

"Let's look at this photo," he said, pointing. "On the left is the Ayatollah Khomeini, president of Iran from 1981-1989, the Supreme Leader who died in July. In the middle is Ayatollah Rafsanjani, the next, and present, president as of August 1989, and Rouhani, probably Iran's future president.

"We've been given information from our overseas correspondents." He paused, hesitated and then said as an aside, "Our reporters, and the *Times,* have informers, and leaks. In any event, we have learned that Ceausescu has scheduled a three-day State visit next week with Rafsanjani, beginning December 18th. We want to get a jump-start on the news before our competitors get the scoop."

He paused again, waited for Anca to comment, which she did not, and then Mr. Curtis continued. "It seems Ceausescu has said that Iran has the best, secret banking system in the world. Especially now, with Rafsanjani as the new president and with his new private bank. We wondered, why did Ceausescu say that? We checked out a lead—about $1 billion dollars in gold. Ceausescu's…"

His assistant came and handed him a note. After reading it, Curtis turned to Anca and said, "We just received word that tanks are preparing to roll through the regions of Banat and Transylvania. What facts can you get for us about *that?*" he asked her.

Anca gave a nervous laugh. "This is all classified information—secret. I can't get any of that."

"From what I know about Romania, a secret is secret to some, but not to all. Maybe you can find a Romanian who's willing to share a *few secrets* with you, and with us."

Curtis closed his heavy folder with a flourish. He was finished with her. Anca packed up her papers while he waited silently. He escorted her to the door. She realized he was her height. She had thought he was taller, or stronger.

Walking next to him, she was wondering who the Romanian was who's willing to share a few secrets with the *Times*.

"Dr. Rodescu." He hesitated. "What do you know about Ceausescu spinning his fortune to gold? What role is Rafsanjani playing with all this?"

"I read about that in yesterday's newspaper," she said, but she didn't answer his questions.

"What will happen to Ceausescu's fortune in Iran if there's a coup against him?"

"I-I can't answer that."

"But that is the question. Readers want to know. This is what sells newspapers."

The elegantly dressed man shook his head in disbelief. "Oh, one more thing," he added. "Perhaps you can help me? The CIA must have a key figure working for them from within the country. Who is it? Whoever they choose, he risks getting killed."

Anca stared at him and she realized, that despite Alec's warnings, she had been right not to cancel her appointment with Curtis. He had given Anca more information than she had given him.

12

TIMISOARA, ROMANIA

> *If only the gods are willing. They rule the vaulting skies.*
> *They're stronger than I to plan and drive things home.*

— HOMER, *THE ODYSSEY*, BOOK 5

"WHERE ARE you going once we get to the depot station?" Father Strancusi asked Petre as the train was nearing Timisoara.

"To the Reverend's house," Petre answered. "They're waiting for me there."

"I'm going to the church. I'll be in the basement." Then he paused and said, "Do you want me to start handing out *our gifts?*"

Petre nodded. No words of explanation were needed. They both eyed each other in agreement as the train stopped for one more security check.

Petre stood up when he heard the sound of heavy boots marching toward their compartment. The tip of a rifle pushed open the door. A soldier as broad as he was tall stepped inside. Every part of his body spoke of physical strength. His black eyes looked as if they were permanently squinting. He had no age; he could have been a youth turned old by his cruelty or an old man made young by his power to kill.

"Show me your papers," he ordered the two men.

Petre wanted to sneer in the soldier's face, but he knew better. Opportunists get angry quickly and can pull a trigger to show off their strength.

"Here," Petre muttered and refrained from throwing his other set of papers at the man.

Suddenly the soldier froze, as if he saw something he couldn't believe. "Custom stamps from foreign countries! How is it possible? No one can travel! Who are you? What are you doing here?" He was clearly suspicious.

"I'm going to inspect the clinic." Petre pointed to his doctor's bag. He was reluctant to defend himself again with his official papers for fear the secret police would contact Central Committee to ask why Ceausescu's doctor was in Timisoara.

"You expect me to believe that? No one from Romania has custom stamps from foreign countries!" He took out a pair of handcuffs. "You're going with me to party headquarters so I can find out who you really are!"

Just then, a heavyset man dressed in a black leather coat approached them. He greeted the guard by name, patted him on the back, whispered something in his ear and offered him a cigarette. He made a joke as he gave the soldier the pack to keep. They both laughed.

"Don't bother with this fool," the man in the long, black leather coat said. "If he wants to travel all day, that's his problem." He spat at Petre's old boots and sneered at him. "Poor slob, looks like a beggar. Get lost! And you too!" he said to Strancusi. He pushed Petre hard and told him to move on.

The soldier didn't interfere. Instead, he took his rifle and pointed it at Petre's head. "Make sure you're on tomorrow's train out of here! I'll be looking for you!"

The second man took Petre's ordinary I.D. card and threw it on the ground. Petre picked it up, took the priest's arm, and calmly pulled his companion away from a group of soldiers who had gathered around them.

"Don't talk," Petre whispered as they walked away. After several minutes, when they were alone and away from the train depot, Petre explained, "The man in the leather coat works for us. We got lucky."

The two men separated, the priest heading toward the church and Petre toward his revolutionaries. As Petre took the path that led toward Mokess's house, he turned his head every few minutes, listening to see if he was being followed.

It was dark, hard to see. The cement sidewalk from the station led to a dirt path. Petre pulled his woolen hat down to cover his ears. Despite the lack of light, he knew the way. Timisoara was the third-largest city in the northwestern region of the country, in the section of Banat. Petre had been going there every few months for two years to confer with Reverend Sandor Mokess.

Walking through the medieval center, he noted several crumbling Baroque buildings. He passed the canal running through town and was struck by a sulphurous smell coming from the nearby chemical factory. The entire area was off limits due to industrial spillage and filth.

Petre approached the Reverend's house and heard shouts of, "Romanians and Hungarians unite!" He moved closer and saw hundreds of people, holding hands. They formed a human chain around the house. Petre walked over to a boy who was standing alone in the cold.

"What's going on?"

"You don't know?" the boy asked, surprised. "Where've you been?"

"I've been traveling all day. Just came from Bucharest."

"Ha, Bucharest, the home of that swine!" And the boy

pretended to vomit. "Don't you have radios in the capital? Aren't we important enough to make news?"

"I'm sure you are." Petre couldn't help but smile.

"Here." The boy raised the volume of a small radio. "There's a report coming from Budapest. They're telling how Ceausescu wants to deport all Hungarians from Transylvania."

"Wait, I hear English," Petre interrupted. "It must be BBC."

The boy handed Petre the radio. Together they walked over to a tree. Petre raised the transistor to their ears and lowered the volume:

"Four masked men armed with clubs and knives broke into the house of Reverend Mokess and beat him up while his three-year-old son and his seven-months' pregnant wife were tied up and forced to watch."

The boy said, "Do you know how Ceausescu silences Hungarians? He trumps up a charge, arrests them, puts them in a cell that has a special irradiation system. He calls the device a Radu. 'G-give that H-hungarian a R-radu,'" the boy imitated Ceausescu with his stammer.' The p-pig will die of p-poison.'"

Petre didn't comment, but the memory of his own father's death remained vivid and painful.

Ceausescu used radiation as a secret weapon to eliminate his enemies. In Munich's Radio Free Europe's Broadcasting offices, there were files about Romanian dissidents who had been irradiated through air condition vents until they succumbed to cancer of the lungs.

In addition, a number of anti-communists on strike against the government were treated in a Bucharest hospital for minor wounds. At the hospital, they were given "so-called X-rays," and within five minutes, they had died.

Radioactive poisoning was Ceausescu's favorite means of

getting rid of a "difficult" person as it left no obvious, physical trace. Murder by poisoning was hard to detect.

"Do you want to hear more?"

The boy raised the volume of his radio.

"I want to hear what the rest of the world will know," Petre told him.

"I know English, too," the boy said proudly. "I dream of going to America."

"First you have important work here." Petre held the radio closer to both of them.

"This is BBC: In Timisoara, near Transylvania, ethnic Hungarians are staging a protest that could turn violent and lead to future unrest in all of Eastern Europe. Here is some background information: In 1940 at the beginning of World War II, Germany oversaw the return of Transylvania to Hungary. But after the war in 1945, the Allies took Transylvania from the Hungarians and gave it back to Romania. This year, the Helsinki Watch accused President Ceausescu of cultural genocide to destroy Hungarian heritage. The ethnic-Hungarian citizens in Timisoara are planning the uprising."

Petre tried to break through the circle of people who were protecting Mokess's house. "I'm sorry," he said, pointing to his doctor's bag. "The Reverend's wife is ill. I must see her." He waved to his colleagues on the stairs. "Tell the people to let me through."

A man with a rifle walked down the steps. "Petre, we've been waiting for you." With his arm, he made a path. "Let the doctor through."

Petre jumped onto the porch, greeted his friends, and entered the modest house. It was just as dark inside as the night outside, for the entire house had one 40-watt light bulb. Petre looked around and spied the thirty-seven-year-old minister. Sandor Mokess wasn't wearing his usual black religious suit. Instead, he was dressed in a brown leather jacket, heavy woolen brown trousers, and brown fur hat.

"You're a popular fellow," Petre greeted his co-leader. And the two men put their arms around each other in understanding of what was ahead.

"I bring good news from Bucharest," Petre said. "I've hand-picked five generals and four politicians to lead the opposition in the capital."

Petre led Sandor to a quiet corner so they could be alone. "One of the politicians is Ileyesco, Ceausescu's right-hand man. But Ileyesco is willing to double-cross the dictator and come to our side."

"I don't trust Ileyesco," Mokess said.

"Neither do I, but for now, we have no choice. He's our link to Gorbachev. The CIA and Gorbachev are working together to get Ceausescu out of Bucharest. We have to follow. Ileyesco can help."

Then Petre outlined the plan:

"The generals and politicians will start agitating in Bucharest as soon as fighting reaches a peak here. Then they'll take Ceausescu to an army barracks. That's where Ileyesco will be invaluable. He'll get Ceausescu's trust, reassuring him that he's being taken to a remote spot for safety. But once there, the generals will take over and stage a trial to convict Ceausescu for crimes against humanity."

"Good. By then, the CIA will be in control here as well as in Bucharest."

Petre and Sandor were very much aware that they were working together to make history.

"I've arranged for your men in Timisoara to get more rifles and machine guns," Petre whispered, and then explained. "I saw Eugen,

Cristina, and Mica last week in Nice. Eugen has a good contact with some arms dealers and Mica has contacts with Romanian government officials. Cristina and Mica are trying to knock down the price. They're insisting that if they pay in cash, they should get two hundred extra machine guns."

"They got us a good deal last month for five hundred rifles," Sandor said.

"Marina Frigidescu pledged ten million dollars for tanks. Eugen negotiated in Nice to get the tanks delivered this week to Timisoara."

"I've received news that the tanks are on their way from Hungary."

"They're moving slowly. During the day, they're hidden inside covered vans. At night, they're covered in barns."

"What about Alec? Has he started transporting the arms through his network?"

"Eugen gave me a list of Alec's contacts. They're all farmers who live in the region."

Sandor laughed. "They're hiding their rifles in haystacks."

Petre nodded and led Sandor to another corner of the room. "Listen, I'm going to get you out of Timisoara when the moment is right. We'll need the dark of a moonless night."

Sandor rubbed his wounded arm. "Yes, it'll be easier for my wife and son to escape when everyone is sleeping. I have to consider their safety."

"Don't worry, I've worked out every detail. Our men will start fighting early Sunday morning, in six days. We'll start the revolution, escape, and then you and I will come back. When the fighting is over, the people will be ready for us to set up a new government. To change from communism to democracy." Petre was calm; he was in control. "We'll leave in the middle of the night. You, me, your wife and son. No one will know."

Then he put his hand on his friend's shoulder. "Sandor, we

can't allow ourselves to be ordinary men. Most men are afraid of suffering or dying. But there are a few of us- like you and me- who see something beyond those fears, something that will live longer than us." He paused. "I hope your wife understands this and won't oppose you."

Sandor nodded, though he was pensive. "Yes," he said. The Reverend tried to convince himself that it would be as easy as Petre believed. But Sandor wasn't sure. He knew from history that no dramatic change of government is quick or smooth. China and Russia were examples—instability was typical after a revolution. Ironically, it's not an easy transition for people to let go of their oppression.

Sandor respected Petre, but he suspected that he had his own ambitions to take over Romania as the next leader. But, he didn't want to criticize him. He had too much respect for Petre.

Instead he said, "I have inside information that Ceausescu will leave for Tehran in a week, despite warnings from his ministers that there's trouble here in Timisoara. He'll leave his wife, Elena, in charge of Romania."

Petre knew that Ceausescu had planned a 3-day State visit, but probably he was more interested in the state of his personal fortune. That's why he had been so nervous when Petre examined him. All he wanted to know was if he was strong enough to travel.

Petre commented, "Ceausescu bragged to me that President Rafsanjani needs Romania for its position on the Black Sea. It's the easiest way to export Iranian oil and gas to all of Europe."

"Yes," Sandor agreed. "Rafsanjani uses politics for economics and economics for his personal gain.

"Listen to this about Rafsanjani," Sandor whispered. "A contact in the Israeli government leaked to me that Rafsanjani is planning to bomb a Jewish community center in Buenos Aires. He'll use a truck filled with explosives and have Hezbollah and Syrian terrorists carry it out. If it succeeds, it would be the worst terrorist attack on Argentine soil."

Both men shook their heads in disbelief. "Buenos Aires had the largest Jewish community center in South America."

"Yes. The Iranians plan to bomb the Israeli Embassy in Buenos Aires as well."

"I understand why they'd use Hezbollah as their proxy terrorists," Petre said. "But why Syrian terrorists?"

"There's an Argentine politician getting ready to be president, Menem, who is in the background. He has Syrian heritage and contacts, and he's anti-Israeli. He'll use Syrian terrorists who live in Argentina, have them work with Hezbollah, and then when president, he'll cover it all up. They'll help him solidify his power."

"Why would Rafsanjani and Iran get involved in all this?"

"Iran wants to punish Argentina for suspending its work with them on nuclear technology," Sandor explained. "Probably, there's a group of Jewish-Argentine scientists working in the nuclear energy sector. I believe they pushed the decision to go against Iran and stop the nuclear program."

"Who advised them to do that?"

"The Mossad. Gave them a signal that a nuclear-strong Iran is dangerous in the Middle East."

"Who advised the Mossad?"

"A group of Argentine priests. There's a Jesuit Archbishop from Buenos Aires who has been working behind the scenes."

"Can this Archbishop be trusted?"

"He's been tapped to be the next Pope. Pope Francis, Jorge Mario Bergoglio, from Buenos Aires."

Petre took Sandor to the far end of the room and spoke softly but urgently. "Sandor, you talk of terrorists.... Remember to send a coalition of men to wipe out the terrorist training camp in the mountains. I've been studying their numbers each day. I estimate there are at least ninety Libyans and Palestinians training in the first valley, 156 kilometers northwest from here. I've told the Americans, but they didn't tell me what they'd do with this information. We can't count on them. You'll have to make sure your men do it. If not, I'll do it myself!"

Sandor made a movement with his eyes in agreement. Petre stopped talking as a man approached Sandor.

Petre walked toward the window to study the crowd. Thousands of people, shouting, yelling, ready to fight. They were just waiting for a signal.

He thought, why didn't I poison Ceausescu in the middle of the night when I had the chance? Why didn't I give him cyanide instead of insulin?

Petre looked at Sandor standing in the middle of his men and said to himself. "His people trust him. He's a man of God. I'm a man of history. Yet am I being arrogant to think history can serve me?"

Petre opened the window and listened to the people chanting. They were waving white flags with words written in red: LIBERTATE! They were yelling, "FREEDOM!"

He remembered how much Ceausescu enjoyed political rallies. He'd raise his arms to the people, like a god, and tilt his black hat to the side as the people cheered him.

Petre understood how powerful a man can feel standing before such a rally. Last week he had been at University Square in Bucharest with Ceausescu, when the leader felt faint and told Petre to take his place. Petre recalled standing on the platform, high above the crowd, holding a microphone, looking down at the mob as they cheered. For just a moment, he imagined they were cheering for him. He felt the blood mount to his head. His heart quickened. There was something thrilling in the moment.

Now again, outside the Reverend's house, he could hear the people cheering for their leader. This time, they were cheering for him; cheering for something only he could give them. He imagined himself in front of a mirror, fixing *his* hat, tilting *his* head before he addressed *his* people. And he saw himself standing on a platform, raising his arms to the sky as the people cheered his name. He would be the man to give his people freedom, a new democracy.

From the pit of his stomach, Petre could feel the temptation to hold power move up toward his lips and fill his smile.

13

NEW HAVEN, CONNECTICUT

"KEN, ARE YOU THERE?" Sandi knocked on the door. "Are you busy?"

Brian, his roommate, opened the door. He smiled and pointed to his friend, who was crouched in a chair soaking his ankle in a bucket of hot water.

"What happened?"

"Practice," mumbled Ken. "But I won the bout."

"Yay!" shouted Sandi. "Did you go for an X-ray?"

"Nah," he said. "Just a strain. Tomorrow I'll be back on the strip."

Sandi walked into the boys' room, which was next door to hers. She leaned against the bookcase and looked around. "This place is a pigsty."

"It's not so bad once you get used to it," said Brian. He was also a fencer, a member of Yale's saber team, the weapon that resembled a cavalry sword. There were three fencing weapons: foil, épée, and saber. Sandi fenced foil.

Sandi came right to the point. "Listen, guys, can you do me a favor?"

"First, what is it, and second, when?" Ken looked at his watch. *"C'est lundi, onze heures du matin.* I've got a French paper to write. Due tomorrow, *mardi,* and I haven't started it yet."

"No, not you, Ken." She turned to Brian. "Ken can't defend me on crutches. But Brian, *you can,*" she said as she smiled.

Sandra liked Brian and enjoyed joking with him. He was cute, with twinkling blue eyes and a cleft chin on a long, thin, six-foot frame.

"What will you do for *me* Sandi?" Brian moved closer to her and put his arm around her waist. She laughed.

"I don't know, cutie. Edit a paper. Freshman Comp."

"Not enough." He winked at her.

She pushed him playfully.

"I do need my laundry done."

Sandi looked at the room—the socks hanging from the dusty venetian blinds, the ripped underwear scattered on the floor. She disliked doing her own laundry, but *this?*

"When do you need it?" She hoped he'd say next week when they'd be home on vacation.

"Tomorrow." Brian opened his closet and showed her a pile of sweaty T-shirts and fencing knickers. "I don't want my mom to think I can't do my own wash."

"I guess I don't have a choice. Okay. Now listen. I need you to come with me to Chapel Street to a journalist's studio. It's about an interview. I want to have the press coverage for when I apply to law school. Just stay in the same room with me and look at me every few minutes like you care about me."

"Some dude wants to make it with ya'?"

"Don't be jealous." She flattened her long, silky blond hair and puckered her lips like a movie star. "He wants to arrange a time for a photo shoot."

Both boys laughed.

"Very funny, guys. Is it so hard to believe?"

"No, no, Sandi. I'm sure you'll make an awesome model." Brian picked up his coat from the floor. "Let's go. This is going to be a blast."

Sandra took a moment to grab her coat and was ready to go.

"I tried to call my mom," she said, "but she wasn't in. I wanted to give her the address." Sandra felt sure everything would be okay and she was adamant—she was going to this meeting, despite her mother's warning her not to.

She was hoping that this first news article could catapult to another, and she'd begin her own publicity that would help for Law school.

"Okay, sport." Brian put his arm around her. "Let's go to this gig."

She turned to him and took his sword. "Oh, I feel so protected."

Sandra wasn't totally joking. She did feel something for Brian, a tingling sensation when he put his arm around her, even in teasing. He was her type: tall, thin, light-hearted, and uncomplicated. Perhaps the way she wished she could be or could have been, if her parents had lived together, or were less complicated themselves.

They walked to the address on Chapel Street. It was a dilapidated building, the only apartment house surrounded by stores, with a buzzer system on the outside porch. Sandra rang as directed, then she and Brian climbed three flights of stairs to find the door half-opened. Once inside, she yelled, "Hello." A man's voice answered, "Take a seat."

It was a sketchy room with no furniture except for two chairs. She and Brian sat down, keeping their coats on.

"Are you there?" Sandra called.

"I'll be a few minutes. I'm on the phone."

Sandra and Brian took some books from their backpacks and started to read. After several minutes, Sandra looked up and shouted, "Should I come back?" She realized this was her chance to give in to reason and leave, yet she didn't feel like retreating.

The room apparently served as studio and sitting room. Three cameras on tripods stood in one corner. Sandra noticed that all three were dusty, obviously not recently used. The lens on the oldest-looking camera was broken, reminding her of an abandoned beach house in winter with broken windows. She buttoned up her coat. There was no heat in the room and very little light.

A man entered the room. He was of medium height, squarely built, muscular, with wide shoulders and a full, black beard. He looked like he spent most of his day working out in a gym. Not at all what she expected in a photographer.

"Can you turn on the lights, somewhere?"

"No, sorry." His apology was perfunctory, and he gave no reason why not. She realized she should get out.

"We've been waiting quite a while," she said. "I think we'd better go, and besides, I have a fencing lesson."

"No. I'd like to take some face photos of you." He moved closer to her. "I want first to interview you. Let's start with your beginnings as a fencer. How did you get involved? Your mother?"

"My mother!" Sandi exclaimed.

Brian put down his book. The room was windowless and it was hard for him to read. Sandra walked toward him and said, "Let's split," but as she moved toward the door, the man blocked her.

"Was your mother a fencer? Did she take you to lessons when working full time? Does she have a lot of friends outside of work?"

"I've had enough of this," Sandra yelled. "I thought you wanted to talk about me, not my mother."

"Yes, of course."

Hearing his accent, Sandra knew he was Romanian. At that moment, she understood why her mother wanted her out of New Haven. She went over to Brian, put her arm around him and calmly placed his arm around her waist. "Let's go, honey."

Brian understood. "Right."

Suddenly, the man ran towards her, yelling. "I haven't finished with you," he yelled as he grabbed her arm, and pulled her down to the floor.

Brian turned and punched the man. As they began to fight, the man took a judo position. In one second, he had punched Brian in the jaw and then thrown Sandi to the floor.

Brian took his fencing saber and used the iron sword to strike the man down. "Sandi! Run!" yelled Brian.

"I can't see where the door is," she screamed. "It's so dark." She fell over an object. It made a huge crash. It was one of the cameras. She picked up the tripod, hit her assailant over the head and ran out the door. Brian followed.

They ran all the way down Chapel Street to York where they stopped at the School of Architecture. They ran inside the building and Brian slammed the door. After a few seconds, Sandra went to the door, opened it a crack, and peeked out. "No one." She went back inside and leaned against the wall next to Brian, her heart pounding.

"Oh my God," she said, horrified, when she turned to look at Brian. "You're bleeding."

"It's okay," he said, his voice shaking. "No broken bones. What about you?"

Her face was red and swollen where the man had slapped her. Brian took his scarf and cleaned her bloody lips and chin.

"What a psycho," Sandra said.

"Yeah, we're lucky we got out alive. Should we tell the police?"

"No." She remembered the professor had written down her name the day before. "Let's forget the whole thing," she said, trying to sound nonchalant. "We don't have time to go through questioning. We've got exams and papers."

At this instant, Sandra became worried about her mother. Was she in trouble, too? Anca had said on the phone that some people were trying to get her attention. I'm glad I'm going home, Sandi thought.

"What do you think that was all about?" Brian asked, examining his swollen jaw in the door's window. "Does he really know your mom?"

"My mom's a pediatrician, not a psychiatrist. How would he know her?" Sandra figured it was easier to keep Brian in the dark with little explanation. She didn't want to scare him. Until she learned from her mother why such menacing things were happening, she couldn't even begin to tell Brian the story. Maybe all these events were meant to be kept confidential.

"He sure looked like a psycho from a Hitchcock movie," Brian said. "Man, he went totally berserk when you moved to the door."

"Yeah. He was freaking out when you used your sword on him." Sandra tried to laugh. "Bravo, Zorro."

"Foiled again. Wham!" Brian started fencing. "*Allez*, attack!" Then he stopped, went over to her and said, "You've got guts, Sandi. You weren't afraid. You're one tough broad."

Sandra wasn't comforted by Brian's awe. She realized that her mother had been right to be worried. Sandra had been wrong to let her curiosity and stubbornness overrule her better judgment. Had this photo shoot merely been a ruse for the bearded man to learn more about her mother? Had Sandra ignored the warning because unconsciously, she wanted to learn more about *Dr. Spy?*

"Do you ever think of your parents while you're at school?" Sandra asked, wanting to talk as she tried to compose herself. She was still shaken up and embarrassed at all that had happened in front of Brian. She should have listened to her mother's warnings.

"No. I'm so busy, I don't have time. But sometimes…"

Sandra interrupted him. She was still nervous. "I think a lot about my parents. They've been divorced for as long as I can remember. My dad has always lived in Romania, and I only have a chance to see him every few months when he goes to a medical conference in Europe. I meet him there, when I can, but I've always been close to my mom."

All kinds of memories she had forgotten came back to her. "My mom made me a photo album for my eighteenth birthday. She put in snap shots for each year of my life, from when I was a baby, and included dozens of photos from my fencing wins, school shows, and awards."

"Yeah, my mom collects things like that, too. I can't believe she displays my fencing trophies on the dining room table. It's embarrassing when my friends come over."

Sandra and Brian laughed. She knew they were both trying to forget what had just happened. She looked at him, his swollen jaw, his bleeding lip. He was pale. She blamed herself. "I'm sorry," she said.

"No problem. I'm fine," he told her, while looking at his scarf full of blood. "This is like a scene from a spy flick—and I love John Le Carré's novels."

He moved closer to her and said, "How cool is it that you have parents who are spies?"

"Who said my parents are spies?"

Even though she was telling Brian that it wasn't true, she wondered what was true. The secret police didn't just go after any Romanian who had emigrated. Not in their own apartment in New York City and not at Yale. Her mother and father worked as doctors, yes, but they had to be involved in something more, something that was now putting all of their lives in danger. Her mother had been adamant about Sandra coming home. It wasn't the usual mother's worrying about a rebellious child.

She moved away from Brian and walked toward the door. "Monsieur Sherlock Holmes. I guess we should go back to the dorm. Safer there."

"Of cour-rse," he answered with a Romanian accent.

She hoped this was the last time she'd hear those words for a while. She couldn't stop thinking to herself, *how did my mom know I was in danger? Is she a spy? Is my father a spy? Are they both Dr. Spy?*

Brian opened the door for her. He noticed she was deep in thought.

"I guess I'll have to do your laundry," she commented.

"That's right, beautiful. Sorry to say, you gotta pay up." He smiled and kissed her goodbye on both cheeks. "The European way. You know," he said, "one day I'd really like to meet your mom."

14

NEW YORK CITY

LE RESTAURANT ST. Barth was squeezed tightly between a Japanese restaurant on one side and a Chinese restaurant on the other. Discreet in its French elegance, the front door was designed with stained glass flowers that were sparkling red and green from the overhead light. A handsome man, tanned and wearing a white suit, opened the door and greeted Anca.

"Bonsoir, Madame."

"Bonsoir, Monsieur." She smiled back and he escorted her into the restaurant.

Anca was surprised and delighted by the elegant room. Antique crystal chandeliers reflected the vases of colored roses on all the tables. She had heard this was the newest restaurant in New York, and a hard reservation to get.

She saw her own reflection in one of the Venetian mirrors and moved toward it to freshen her lipstick. Despite her age, forty-two, Anca looked much younger.

Another young man greeted her, smiling. *"Bonsoir, Madame.* May I help you?" He reached out to take her coat.

"*Je vois quelqu'un m'attend.* Someone is waiting for me." She looked in the direction of the bar and waved to Alec.

"*Ah, oui,* he's talking to the owner."

She noticed the men were engrossed in conversation and walked over to the long zinc bar. Quietly, she sat next to Alec, smiled hello, and helped herself to some cheese and crackers that had been set out on a plate.

While Alec was busy talking, she surveyed the restaurant. Dozens of vases were filled with roses of all colors and scattered through the rooms. There was a sweet fragrance as if she was in the middle of a garden, *un jardin extraordinaire.*

One small candle stood next to each vase in a specific design, so that the soft flame would warm the flowers and enhance their aroma. Every table was a display of beautiful people, well-dressed, jeweled and stylishly coiffed. They were the movers and shakers of New York City, and they were all pleased to dine together as if the restaurant had been created for their private fun.

There was a buzz in the room.

Anca noticed a woman at a table directly in the center of the large room, apparently dining alone. She had a red-dyed mink coat draped around her shoulders, although there was no chill in the air. She wore her black hair in a chignon that looked as if it had been planted on the top of her head like a bird's nest. She had a Bic pen in her hand and was writing in a small notepad. From time to time, she'd look at the door to see who had entered the restaurant and then she'd jot down something on her notepad. She'd turn her bird-nest head from left to right and listen to conversations drifting from tables nearby. She'd return to writing in her notepad and continue the same routine again and again. Must be a society journalist, Anca thought.

A heavy woman, moving slowly in her three-inch heels, approached the bird lady's table and they kissed cheek to cheek.

Anca recognized her from the newspapers—something about a trial, insider trading, or taxes.

Then her thoughts were interrupted. "Anca," Alec greeted her as if he had just realized she was sitting next to him. "You're looking beautiful. This is Jean-Pierre. We were talking about Romania. The French are interested in Romanian politics."

"*Mais oui, nous sommes des frères. Ça m'intéresse beaucoup.* It's a Latin country like ours. So many Romanians live in Paris."

"You mean you're waiting to get a head start there in business or real estate once the communists leave," Alec smiled.

"Ah, *mon ami*, why must you be so suspicious? There is more to life than business." Jean-Pierre's beautiful suit, suntan and pink sapphire pinky ring belied his words.

Alec laughed. "Life has taught me that first you must be practical in your business, and then you can live."

Alec knew what he was saying. Years ago, as the chief engineer at the Ministry of Agriculture in Ceausescu's government, he had escaped Romania two months after Anca did.

Once he arrived in the United States, Alec continued to dedicate his life to helping others in New York and created a foundation for Romanian artists. In reality, it was his way to stay in the midst of politics. He told acquaintances that he had retired from business, but Anca knew that wasn't true. Often, she would ask him, "What do you *really do?*" He would respond with a wave of his foulard. "I try to be useful."

"Come, my dear," he said as he took Anca's arm to lead her to their table. "Let's eat. I'm hungry."

"I'm sorry I'm late."

"Quite all right, *chérie*. Jean-Pierre served me some pâté at the bar." He patted her hand like a father, even though he was just eight years older than she.

Jean-Pierre walked over to the maître d'. "Give them a bottle of Château Margaux." He turned to Alec. "*Compliments de la maison.*"

The waiter approached the table. "Good evening. Would you like to start with a cocktail?"

Anca answered, "A Chivas. On the rocks."

"Be careful," Alec warned.

"I need something strong."

"Maybe you'll have reason to celebrate," he said. "The editorial board of the *Times* assured me they won't print anything yet about Romania."

"How do you know all that? I just met with Jon Curtis this morning."

Alec smiled and took her hand. "My dear, he's a friend of mine. I offered him more information than you did." Alec took a sip of his kir royale.

"Let's toast to your *secrets*," she said.

They raised their glasses. "*Noroc.* Cheers."

Alec began. "I told Curtis he could write an article based on my information that has to do with the friendship of Ceausescu with the Iranian president, Rafsanjani, if he waits a while before printing anything about Romania."

"Why do you want the *Times* to wait?"

Alec took a sip of his drink. "I want to keep Romania, and Petre, out of the limelight for now."

Anca dropped her bread. She was annoyed that Alec was interfering in her work with the *Times*. As far back as she could remember, Alec was always protecting Petre. *Why?*

"Petre is a very important man these days." Alec looked at the table to the left of them and then to the right. Reassured he could talk safely, he moved closer to her. "A key figure in Romania's future."

"Is Petre the person Curtis thinks is working for the CIA from inside Romania?"

Alec didn't answer.

She took a sip of scotch.

"What happens if the Americans and Russians use Petre to start an uprising and then get rid of him?" she asked. "Then put their own man in?"

Alec nodded, also showing concern. "I'm sure he's aware of the danger. He can control the people up to a point. Their allegiance can be short-lived."

She drank her glass of scotch too quickly and looked for the waiter to order another one.

"You know, I haven't talked with Petre for more than ten minutes every few months, and always just to discuss the logistics of Sandi meeting him. He'd ask about me and I'd ignore the question. I resented the fact that he never asked me *not to sign* the divorce papers. 'You might as well be completely free,' he told me."

She brought her hand down sharply on the table. "I haven't been free of him for one minute in nineteen years. He was fully aware that when he hid me in your tractor, he'd never join me."

Alec put his hand on her shoulder to calm her. "I want you to know that I found another defective tractor for him. I had all the papers ready. In the end he said no. So, I took the tractor instead.

"Try to understand. Petre thought communism could be brought down in months. He never imagined it would take so many years. Perhaps it was poor judgment. Perhaps he made a mistake as a young idealistic man. Whatever. The bottom line is that he did believe that after a necessary delay, he'd join you in New York and until he could, he wanted to protect you and the baby."

"He never asked me what I wanted."

"Try to be reasonable. He was part of a group determined to overthrow the dictator from the very beginning. That's why he went to America in the first place. When he met Ceausescu in Washington, he jumped at the chance to become his doctor."

"He kept all this a secret from me. Never shared this with me.

His political work was always more important than me." She stopped talking and closed her eyes, feeling her face grow warm.

Then she continued, "Looking back, I wonder if he used me as a decoy in Transylvania to take attention away from him. Was that part of his master plan?"

"Petre did you a favor to get you out."

"A favor? *He got rid of me so he could start a revolution!*"

"He gave you and Sandra a new life; a better life."

"I'm sick of everyone praising him. What about me? He sacrificed my happiness for his own ambitions."

"Don't judge him so harshly."

"Petre stayed in Romania for many different reasons. He had his ambitions, too. It was not only about avenging his father's death."

"I would disagree with that, Anca. He stayed to fulfill his dream to help Romania change into a democracy."

"I had dreams, too. I wanted to be a researcher in infectious diseases. I didn't have a choice. I was pregnant, and his CIA friends put me in the department of pediatrics where they had contacts. I was just another piece of the puzzle to fit in somewhere. Professionally and privately."

Alec took her hand. "Listen, I think Petre's work is coming to an end. He and Eugen have been working for years to overthrow Ceausescu. Eugen from Western Europe, Petre from within Romania. Cristina is marrying Eugen now because she believes his work is over. Yes, Cristina is involved, and Marina and Mica, too."

Anca brought her open hand down on the table again. She had suspected that her friends were doing something behind her back. Angry, and a little drunk, she said, "They're behind a revolution and they never told me a thing. I'm their best friend."

"They didn't want you to suffer any more than you have. They wanted to protect you."

"*Protect me?* I'm being harassed. The Romanian secret police are after me in order to put pressure on Petre. The mother of his child —and his child, too."

"The end is near," Alec warned.

"Not my end. I have a plan. I believe Petre will have a problem and I can help him."

"What are you talking about?" Alec sounded angry at her defiant tone.

"Let's change the subject."

She didn't want to tell him about her plan for the coming weeks. She had considered telling him about Evdochia's phone call, to ask him if he knew what it meant. Then, she changed her mind, angry that he and her friends were cutting her out of important happenings. Instead, she said, "I'd rather discuss my meeting with Curtis. Maybe you can give me the information he wants from me?"

"I told you yesterday that I'm getting you away from the *Times*. I told that also to Mr. Curtis." Alec was angry at his dinner companion. "*You're out with the Times!*" he whispered angrily in her ear. "You should have never started with them or with Voice of America."

"Why should you decide what I'm to do?"

"What can I do with you, Anca, my dear? You must stop getting involved with politics."

"I can't. Politics is involved with me, like it is with you," she said as she gave him a forced smile. "So, tell me, what do you think? Curtis is fascinated by the friendship of Ceausescu with the Iranians—Rafsanjani in particular."

"A future problem," Alec agreed, and then he paused. "What will I do with you, Anca? You're so stubborn. You're like a rebellious child. I'm warning you. No more politics." He shrugged, but he understood her interest, and he answered.

"Ceausescu is helping Iran build nuclear facilities underground. Rafsanjani is his contact man."

"In caves? Isn't that the same thing the Pakistanis do?" she remembered that Curtis had mentioned Ali Bhutto. She knew the Egyptians and Turks did the same. Caves—lots of them in that region. It's easy to dig inside soft limestone.

"Yes. The Pakistanis wanted their own nuclear bomb built in a facility hidden underground. After India tested their first atomic bomb in 1974, Pakistan was outraged. It was then that Ali Bhutto, the prime minister, met with Ceausescu to discuss using Romanian-style caves. Bhutto was competing with India who had atomic energy first, and told his people, 'We will eat grass or leaves, even go hungry, but we will get one of our own.'

"It's not a coincidence that Bhutto got his number one nuclear scientist, Dr. Abdul Khan, involved. Bhutto arranged for Khan to work in Holland for the same nuclear company, URENCO, where Ceausescu had also sent one of his spies to work, but to the German branch. Dr. Khan, once working in the Netherlands, married a Dutch woman.

"It's not a coincidence that Dr. Khan returned to Pakistan with everything he learned during his time at URENCO, including his wife and blueprints of centrifuges that he stole or bought. Just as Ceausescu's agent did—set up a nuclear facility in Transylvania. Bhutto built Khan an institute in Islamabad. Who knows at this point where Dr. Khan has sold his stolen blueprints? North Korea?"

"North Korea?" Anca asked. "Curtis spoke of that, too. I had commented that it could take North Korea *several generations to build up a nuclear arsenal.*"

"Yes," Alec nodded. "It started almost twenty years ago, when Kim invited Ceausescu to North Korea in 1971. The research you shared with Curtis is correct."

They both smiled. Anca felt triumphant.

"Ceausescu went again to North Korea several years later and received a red-carpet reception. The two rogue leaders discussed how Ceausescu could help Kim begin a nuclear program. Talks continued and in May 1978, Kim Il-Sung came *by train* to pick up nuclear parts in Bucharest.

"Many people had asked why Kim traveled so far by such a slow means of transportation? Of course, he had a reason. He paid his respects to Comrade Ceausescu with trunks filled with gold and left with a train full of parts for nuclear bombs."

Anca picked up her glass and poured herself some wine. "I imagine Ceausescu wanted the North Korean dictator as a client before Bhutto and Dr. Khan got him."

Alec nodded in disgust. "Ceausescu, the communist, made more money than any American CEO. Soon it will all be over: the terrorist training camp, the secret nuclear facility, everything destroyed. Ceausescu, too."

"Wow! I've known you all my life and never dreamed you were involved with such dealings." She drank her wine, then poured herself some more, and didn't speak until she had finished the glass.

Alec said, "All this is confidential."

"Actually, Curtis spoke of a leak to the *Times* about Ceausescu going to Tehran to deposit gold in Rafsanjani's bank." She smiled at Alec. "Is it possible that you gave the leak?"

He smiled back at her, but then his smile turned downward. He moved closer to her, and said in a low voice, "Yes. To the *Times* and to Curtis, personally."

"Why did you do that? It must be secret information. Classified."

"You're right. I'm hoping the Romanians will read about it in the *Times*. That's exactly what will make them get even more crazy against Ceausescu. It will be the last straw. They starve and suffer their entire lives and he gets so rich that he hides a billion dollars of gold that he doesn't even need."

"So why this leak, now?"

"It'll make the Romanians fight harder to get rid of Ceausescu. Money and gold are personal motivators." He pointed his finger at her in warning. "I'm telling you this because you're my dearest friend, and also because I want you to realize how dangerous this is and that you shouldn't be getting involved in any of it."

"I'll never repeat anything." Anca raised her hand to swear. She poured herself another glass of wine. "For my secrecy, I want a favor."

"A *favor?*"

"Yes," she said emphatically.

He smiled with the boyish grin he had used since he worked with her father and had a secret from her.

"First me," he teased. "I have a favor from someone and I forgot yesterday to satisfy the request. I apologize. I've been preoccupied. Let me give you something *secret* and special before you ask me for your *favor.*"

"Why do you enjoy speaking to me in riddles?"

He laughed and took from his pocket a small velvet jewelry box. "Petre gave me this for you."

She opened the box, stared at the contents, and remained speechless.

"I saw him recently. He moved into a new apartment and found some of his mother's belongings when packing. He said you'd understand."

"His mother's earrings. She wore them all the time."

Anca showed him a pair of dainty filigree gold circles with a small square emerald in the middle. "He loved his mother very much. He lost her when he was fifteen years old to bone cancer. She was in a lot of pain."

Alec took his foulard and wiped Anca's tears.

She put on the earrings, stroked them, and poured herself another glass of wine. When she finished, she moved to refill her glass. Alec took the wine bottle away from her.

"You've had enough. You didn't tell me what's the favor you want from me?"

"It's about Petre."

The waiter came over to their table and interrupted their conversation. "*Monsieur-dame,* have you decided what you'd like to order?"

"Do you have any specials?" Alec asked.

"*Oui. Escalopes de veau viennoise.*"

"Sounds good. Anca, what do you think?"

Anca didn't hear him. She only heard *Viennese.* Her thoughts involuntarily went back to that first day in Vienna after escaping Romania in the tractor. She had realized then that Petre worked for the CIA.

"Alec," she said, refilling her glass of wine and slurring his name, "The favor... Can you phone Petre? You must promise not to say that I asked you. Just say you saw me at a party."

She stopped talking. She wiped her sweaty forehead with a napkin. Alec looked at her, moved his chair closer, and put his arm around her shoulders.

"*Tell him I have a plan,*" Anca wanted to finish her sentence, but instead, she placed her arms on the table and leaned her cheek on her hands. Wine mixed with scotch had taken its toll.

15

NEW YORK CITY

AFTER DINNER, Anca asked Alec to drop her off at her office in the hospital. He insisted he'd help her go home to bed, but stubbornly, she told him she was feeling better. He asked if he should wait for her and take her home when she finished. Again, she said no, and he reluctantly agreed.

Anca entered her office, intending to review some patients' charts before meeting Mark in the morning. Instead of selecting the charts, she took a pile of handwritten letters from Petre out of her desk drawer. The one on the top was the most recent.

Petre had been meeting their daughter in Vienna or Budapest every few months from the time that Sandra had been ten years old. Before each trip, he'd call Anca to discuss the details of the schedule and the logistics. At the end of the conversation, he'd change his tone to a softer one and ask about her: "How are you? What are you doing?"

Anca never answered, although she wanted to. Stubbornly, she cut the conversation and answered in a monotone to discuss their daughter. Her resentment cut their line of communication to the essentials.

After each vacation, Petre wrote Anca a letter, reporting on what he and Sandra did, what they saw, and how she reacted. There was always a paragraph or two with his personal reflections. In his last letter after their time in Budapest, he had commented on how grown up Sandra looked and how strange it was to think that she was starting college. He was being nostalgic. "Where did the time go? What would have happened to the three of us if we had all stayed together in Romania?"

Anca never answered his letters. He also sent her birthday cards and included photos of his vacations with Sandi, sharing how much their daughter was enjoying their travels.

Yet often, in the quiet of her office, when she was alone, Anca read and reread his letters and cards. She even studied his handwriting to see if life had changed his penmanship. Once, she thought about taking some pages and cards to a friend who claimed she could analyze handwriting. Then Anca changed her mind. She was afraid to find out if Petre appeared different in someone else's eyes.

When Sandra became interested in photography, Anca gave her a pocket Kodak so she could take pictures on her vacations. Anca's real motive was to see pictures of Petre, not just of Sandi or landmarks. Anca was curious to see how life had changed him.

Or, if she could see on his face whether or not he still loved her.

This evening, all alone in her office, lightheaded from the wine and scotch, but no longer woozy and heavy-hearted from talking with Alec about Petre, she picked up his last letter. He had eliminated the travelogue and had gone straight to the point. She touched the page as if it were his skin.

3 September 1989

My Dearest Anca,

I have just put Sandra on the plane. As I waved goodbye, I felt sad, as she reminded me so much of you. I saw you in her, and I was taken back to when you left our village and said farewell. You were just a little older than Sandra is now. I can still see your fiery eyes.

Despite the passage of time, I know you will always be angry at me for not joining you in Vienna or New York as I had promised. I can't blame you for not forgiving me, even though my deepest wish is that one day you will understand that the pain I caused you was not my intent. I had hoped to protect you, not hurt you. If I had been truthful with you from the beginning, you would have never left Romania.

The timing was perfect for you to escape to safety. I had to let you go. They would have arrested you and tortured you in Romania. I feared you would have lost the baby, our beautiful Sandi.

I had no choice, Anca, but to lie to you. How could I have told you the truth when you said you'd only go if I promised to follow? How could I have kept you in this Inferno while knowing your chance to escape to America would never come again?

Over the years, I have tried to justify my actions. I had the revolution. I knew I could never be happy until I achieved my goal. Yet I truly believed that I and my group could change the government within months, and then I'd be able to join you in New York. I never imagined the revolution would take so many years to happen. I had miscalculated. Misjudged. I made the worst mistake of my life to let you go away from me.

Please, Anca, don't judge me harshly. I have suffered every day, every night because of what I did. I suffer by living without you.

I knew you had your career. You were always a compassionate and capable doctor. I knew you would be successful. You had the baby—our love.

I realized you would have difficulties in a foreign country, but I was sure you would make a good life for yourself in New York with friends from Romania to support you.

What I didn't want to think about was that eventually you would forget me and find someone else who would love you. Someone who would know how special you are.

My real motive for letting you go, and you must believe me, was for our child. So, our child would be able to live, to live and grow up in a free world with all its opportunities. I did it for Sandi.

Now when I see her, almost a woman, with the glow of youth in her eyes and your beauty and passion, I believe my decision was right. I think of the suffering you have endured so she would grow up to be happy and secure in a world that could never be yours. I thank you, Anca, for what you did without me, for all your sacrifices.

If God should decide that I should never see you again, please know that I have always loved you. I have never stopped loving you. If I should give my life for the ideals of freedom and revolu-

tion, the one thing I am happy about is that I was able to give you a child. The most important achievement in my life has been that my child's mother is you. My daughter has before her a woman who has heart and courage.

I knew when you left me, you'd never return to me. I had no other choice. I beg you to forgive me. I want you to know I love you and always will.

Petre

For several weeks after Anca received this letter, which read to her as a farewell, she couldn't concentrate on her work. During the day, she'd pretend Petre was near. In her mind, she'd talk to him, confess her secret thoughts, reminisce about their life together, and, above all, forgive him. At night, she'd dream of him. She'd wake up excited, having imagined their lovemaking, fantasizing he was caressing her skin and kissing her breasts, their bodies becoming one.

When she couldn't sleep, she tried to relive all their nights of love. She could almost feel the cold floor under their naked bodies, the blazing fireplace, the smell of wood and passion. She remembered how they would roll together on the bearskin rug and Anca would giggle when the bear's cold nose rubbed against her bare skin. Petre moved on top of her and warmed her with his own nose, wiggling it on her face, on her stomach, and on her thighs. He would play with her, laugh, tease her, and hold her away until she begged him to come closer. She would pull him into her, grab his back, and dig her nails into his skin. "Deeper, deeper," she implored. "More, more. I love you so much."

One night, she broke her oath and wrote to him, telling him that she understood and forgave him. She was being selfish by remaining resentful for so many years. She had been wrong to deprive the three of them from enjoying a united family.

When morning came and cooled her trembling skin, she put the letter away and didn't mail it.

Yet recently, in the middle of a sleepless night (morning for Petre in Bucharest) she telephoned him, as she did after her vision of him in Paris, but he wasn't home. Then, night turned to day, and sick patients called her back to reality. She didn't telephone again.

It was during this time that she became more distant with Mark. Her attitude toward him became erratic, as if she transferred her conflicting feelings about Petre to Mark. She had a long list of excuses of why she had to work late, see patients in the evening, and sleep at her own apartment. She couldn't tell Mark why she wanted to be alone. She felt guilty. He in turn misunderstood; he thought she was going through a difficult time because Sandra was leaving for college. He was always ready to forgive Anca. She knew he loved her very much and looked away so as not to see the truth.

The autumn of 1989 passed. Warm days turned cold. Anca's dreams of love making with Petre subsided. Her attempts to phone him were suppressed. Her relationship with Mark turned into a partnership as they tried to help sick patients and confront unanswered questions about pain and death. Often, she wished she could give Mark more. She had tried, but could not, and felt sorry.

To lose herself, or perhaps to keep Petre from haunting her, she worked harder. In addition to seeing patients, teaching, and coordinating the clinic with students and interns, there was broadcasting and consulting for the *Times*. Then she started to be harassed.Anca reread Petre's last letter—his apology and confession. She felt a thumping on her head, as if soldiers were marching on her brow and poking their rifles into her eyes. She tasted the wine and bitter scotch on her lips. How awful, she thought. I've never done that before. She remembered her dream—ominous, a warning. Petre climbing the mountain. She had awakened in fright and had to run to the bathroom to vomit. She felt sick, yet she had no fever or symptoms. She had been nauseous because she felt danger. It was a panicky sensation that turned physical as if it were a virus. She didn't know how to cure it.

Why did she tell Alec she believed Petre would have a problem and she could help? Was it because of Evdochia's phone call?

She wondered if it was because of "woman's intuition" that she felt a pull toward Petre? Perhaps it was her maternal instinct to take away the danger surrounding him. It was strange, as she didn't even know what kind of danger he was in.

In the past few days, she had tried to gather clues to assess Petre's situation. She had spoken to various people who had revealed what they knew without their realizing she was searching for information: Evdochia, Cristina, Marina, Mica, Alec, and even Curtis. All of them had given her pieces of the puzzle. She believed that the clues were not coincidental.

As she pondered the months' events, she fingered the earrings Pete had given her. When had he seen Alec, and why? Why did Petre want her to have the earrings now? He had had them for years. What had Petre been doing in Paris last spring? Had she really seen him, or had the fog played with her imagination?

Anca was trying to piece together the clues. She realized they were helping her decide how and when to implement her plan: She would leave New York and find Petre, no matter how difficult that might be.

Anca had worked hard to get where she was. Becoming a doctor in New York had taken strength. She had spent years repeating her medical training in America and taking her exams all over again. She had raised Sandra alone. Her determination to be strong was also her weakness. It had stripped her of personal freedom—the very freedom that Petre had wanted to give her. To be obsessed by the desire to create a new life meant that she couldn't do or see or be anything else. For all these years, she had been programmed like an arrow, aimed at her target, to work hard and succeed. She was no different from Petre, Cristina, Marina, Mica, Alec and all the Romanian revolutionaries, fated or cursed, driven to live only for their goal.

Her goal was now to find Petre. She could not, and would not, say goodbye forever to him.

She stood up and went to her file cabinet. Opening the bottom drawer, she took out an envelope yellowed with time. The two men in Vienna, the same ones who had helped her once she'd made her escape, had given her an American passport and multiple documents. In the last paper was a telephone number in Washington, D.C. They had told her to use it if she ever needed to get in touch with them.

PART III

REIGN OF TERROR

DECEMBER 17-26,1989

Penelope's Archery Challenge to Odysseus, Theodor van Thulden 1600s

16

TIMISOARA, ROMANIA

AFTER A WEEK OF DISCUSSIONS, Petre Ilianu was ready and excited to put into motion what he and his group had planned for years. They had all agreed that they'd start at the Romanian Orthodox Cathedral in Timisoara's main square. It reminded him of another church, many years ago in Bucharest when he was thirteen years old. His father had taken him to see a wooden icon of Saint Irena; she had been crying real tears.

Petre had not been inside a church since then. This morning, people had forced open the cathedral's doors and he had entered with them. Kneeling down to pray for strength, he felt sure that God had chosen him to bring freedom to Romania.

Unknown to the people as their leader, he left the church and walked through Opera Square toward the Bega River.

Biting wind pierced his chest while snowflakes covered his old coat. He heard a series of explosions and walked toward the noise. A student rebel had started an outcry by throwing Molotov cocktails in the middle of the square. Another protester joined him and shot several policemen who were hiding in a bus. Another rebel threw a bomb at the bus.

Petre saw a group of women running into the square, waving the familiar Romanian flag, but with the communist star in the middle cut out. He stared at a woman who had the torn pieces in her mouth and was moving to the crowd. "Don't be violent. *Fara violenta!*" she was screaming.

The women roared back, "Don't stop us! *Libertate!*"

He knew the mob wouldn't listen.

"Securitate agents are coming!" someone yelled.

"The secret police! Take cover—they're shooting!"

A man ran into the street and then darted back into a broken-down building. Returning with a torch, he lit the boarded up doors and threw a bomb into the flames.

Romania's bloody revolution had begun.

The crowd numbered in thousands; yet it was hard to tell who was on which side. Former communists turned anti-communists overnight to join the rebels, but were called collaborators and then chased by the mob.

One man shouted, "Who's with us?" Another voice screamed, "Who knows?" Students signaled that the army had changed sides and was now marching alongside them. Everyone except the secret police and Iranian Revolutionary Guards that Rafsanjani had given Ceausescu were fighting against the dictator.

Petre heard more gunfire, and then air-raid sirens. Tanks rolled into the square with men he had selected himself. They were shooting Ceausescu's guards.

He continued moving through the mob to assess the rebellion's progress. A voice from a loudspeaker shouted, "Go home! Get away from the square!" It was a warning from the secret police before they stormed out of armored cars and attacked the rebels with iron chains and steel pipes.

An old man in the street was being beaten by the police. The people watched, outraged as the man was shoved down to the hard concrete and blood poured from his head.

They shouted, "No more!" But the police didn't stop, banging their steel pipes on anyone near. Violence intensified—hatred mixed with passion. There was no stopping the hysteria from the police and crowd.

A woman carried a wooden stick in her hand. She was running toward a Securitate agent to strike him down. He grabbed her coat, clubbed her with his steel pole, and beat her to death. The snow turned blood red.

Petre watched, horrified. The suffering and fury of the people became his own. He wanted to grab the Securitate agent and strangle him. Instead, fixed on his bigger role, he raced to the church where the priest was handing out guns. A line of people extended far into the street. Today, the people were queuing up for ammunition. They were ready to fight back.

Petre took the steps down to the church basement and found the priest. "Make sure each person shows you their I.D. before you give them a gun. Check their photos."

Petre left the church and ran to the Bega River where a group of students were throwing portraits of Ceausescu into bonfires. He watched as fire ate the smile that had deceived 23 million people for 24 years.

He also saw a group of students breaking windows in a bookstore. They grabbed books off shelves and threw them onto a fire to burn dictators' tales: *The Communist Manifesto* and *Das Kapital.*

The Securitate rushed in, shooting into the crowd as the flames roared. The rebels kept coming, filling the square. It appeared as if the entire population of Timisoara was in the streets. Young and old together shouted, "We are united! Down with Ceausescu! Down with corruption!"

Petre joined them as they marched from Opera Square to Union Square to Liberty Square. They were shouting that the Romanians should take note of how communism had crumbled in

East Germany, Poland, Yugoslavia, Hungary, Bulgaria, Czecho-slovakia, and especially the U.S.S.R.

As the wave of protest continued to roar, anarchy broke out in front of the Communist Party headquarters. Petre saw three buses, each with drawn curtains, stop in a parking lot. Securitate police rushed out of the buses and opened fire on the crowd. They used tear gas and water cannons.

He quickly gave a signal to his men to counterattack. Hundreds of his rebels overturned the buses and smashed the exteriors with clubs. Then they toppled a seven-foot concrete statue of Ceausescu and kicked it with their boots.

One of Petre's men led the mob toward the edge of town. There, Petre stood atop a hill, waiting to signal to a group of miners to enter the square. They were ready with smeared soot and grime on their faces, looking like hell hounds descending on Earth. They wore helmets with yellow lights that guided their way as hundreds of them raged through the streets, marching five abreast. Students walked next to them, blowing whistles, while women carried candles and chanted for freedom.

More and more miners entered the city and more and more people marched with them. Armed with steel pipes and chains, the miners smashed store windows, overturned parked cars, and clubbed anyone in their way. People cheered them on with a fury that linked them together. "We are united! *Libertate!*"

Petre looked at his people, marching, and protesting. He was proud of their spirit to fight and to tolerate no more injustice.

"We will be free!" he yelled through his bullhorn. It was all happening as he had hoped, a revolution that he and his group had planned for years.

By early evening, Petre led the masses from Liberty Square toward Mokess's house. Thousands of Romanians demonstrated with the Hungarians, Germans, and Serbs who lived in Timisoara. Huddled together, they sang the national anthem as if they were in church and God was their witness.

Reverend Mokess came out of his house and with his fingers in a V-sign, raised his arms. "My Brothers, I have not worked alone. The real hero of the revolution has been silent for more than twenty years. The moment has come to pay him homage. I want you to know who he is."

Mokess went into the crowd and led Petre up the stairs. The people stared at the stranger. Petre waved from the balcony but didn't say a word.

Mokess spoke for him, using Petre's bullhorn, "Cheer for Petre Ilianu, the true hero of the revolution. Our leader!"

The people yelled, "Petre! Petre!"

He waved, satisfied. He had them in his hands. They would allow him to continue his work.

17

TRANSYLVANIA, ROMANIA

AT MIDNIGHT, Petre approached his most loyal lieutenant, Dan, and told him, "Choose fifty of our best men to go with me to the western ridge of the mountains."

"When should they be ready?" Dan asked, taking off his black-framed eyeglasses.

"In an hour. I want to get to the terrorist camp before sunrise."

"What else do you need?"

"A full supply of dynamite, hand grenades, missiles, and rocket launchers. Get the men to load them into the jeeps."

"I'll get you everything you need. I'm coming, too."

Petre and Dan led the convoy of jeeps to a secluded area where they could park and approach the camp on foot. They had traveled four and a half hours during the night. It was still dark. Petre looked at his watch—5:30 a.m.

"We'll have to do a complete blitz just at the time of their dawn prayer," he whispered to Dan. "We'll catch them unaware."

Petre took out his high-powered night binoculars and studied the terrorist camp. "Two Alouette helicopters," he whispered, passing Dan the binoculars. "Look—two o'clock. Three Mirage airplanes. Ceausescu has suicide pilots. We have information that the Romanian instructors are teaching the Palestinian pilots who were given to Ceausescu by Arafat, how to fly, but not how to land."

Dan studied the surrounding area. "Look at their practice targets—three o'clock."

Petre took the binoculars back. An American flag was pinned at the center of each target. Bullet holes had pierced the stars. He continued studying every angle of the compound's five acres.

"This training camp is just the beginning," he said. "When the terrorists leave here, they'll each form their own cell. There must be thirty to forty of these terrorist cells in Austria, Germany, Holland, Italy, France, Spain, and England. There will be more."

Suddenly Petre adjusted his binoculars. "I don't like what I see."

"What is it?"

"Two buildings—garages—with several tanks separating them. They look like tin shacks. I've heard that the terrorists are working on a nuclear fission device known as a dirty bomb. It's an explosive packed with uranium and radioactive debris that contaminates a large radius.

"Hand me the other binoculars—the special ones that can see interiors," Petre said, as he studied the two tin buildings and described what he was seeing.

"The one on the left contains the dirty bombs. The building on the right contains Kalashnikov rifles. Let's target the building on the right so we don't disperse radioactive material from the dirty bombs. The tanks between the buildings will be our buffer."

Petre spoke into his walkie-talkie to his lieutenant. "Have your men point their rifles at nine degrees southeast. That's the tin building on the right. Verify when that they have that location on their equipment." He waited for the confirmation and then continued. "At the count of three, blast all rocket launchers. One, two, three!"

There was the sound of bombs, cries, screams, and then the sight of a fire blazing. Petre studied the black sky as it turned red. Then he turned to Dan and calmly announced, "They're destroyed."

Dan pointed his finger toward a long building at the far end of the camp that looked like barracks. "A group of men are coming out to assess the damage. It's eight minutes before six o'clock." Dan studied his watch. "Sunrise today is six oh five."

"We'll have to hurry to get to the institute before them. The bombing has warned them we're here." Petre focused his binoculars on several long lines of men bent in prayer despite the devastating blast. Bowing toward Mecca in the east, they swayed back and forth.

Petre and Dan ran down the hill to their jeep. Within a minute, the entire convoy of jeeps followed and together they began their descent. Petre picked up his hand radio and informed them, "We're not finished. Follow me to our next target."

As Dan drove, Petre thought of his men; he was concerned for their safety. He hoped he wasn't pushing their luck. Everything had been going smoothly until now. He feared the terrorists had been apprised of the attack and were preparing a counter offensive at the nuclear institute. In addition, packs of wolves and wild boars indigenous to Transylvania roamed the hills in the area. Petre radioed his men to put silencers on their rifles and to be on extra alert.

The American government had told Petre that they'd prefer to strike the institute by air, but Petre asked the CIA to give him a chance to strike first by land with his men. There would be fewer civilian casualties and less collateral damage, he had calculated. After several meetings when he was last in Budapest, his group reluctantly agreed, and gave approval for him to lead a Special Forces team to attack the nuclear institute first by foot.

Petre explained to Dan what was inside the institute.

"Romania makes high-tech centrifuges. They are very tall, made of steel, and in the shape of round hollow tubes about two meters in diameter. They have special rotors that spin at supersonic speed to purify natural uranium into bomb fuel. This type of enriched uranium is the most difficult to produce. Romania has A-quality uranium and plutonium for the most modern centrifuges to produce nuclear bombs. Romania bought extra heavy water, clandestinely from Norway, to be used as a coolant."

He stopped talking. Their jeep skidded going up the narrow mountainous path and zigzagged on some rocks. Petre was concerned they might hit a landmine. He stared hard at the road ahead of them, searching for any type of trap.

"We're getting close," Dan said, giving the jeep more gas to make the climb. "The institute is three kilometers from here on top of the northeastern peak at one o'clock."

Petre looked around. The rising sun colored the mountains red in the east. With a heavy heart, he wondered if it were an omen of blood.

Dan turned to him. "Where did the Romanians get so much money to set up this facility? It's so high-tech."

Petre eyed the solar energy installation. Satellite dishes of all sizes lined the mountain peak. "Oil money. Gaddafi supplies the cash. Ceausescu supplies the scientists and the hidden site. Arafat supplies the clients, like North Korea and Iran. What do these clients provide? They set up a nuclear bazaar for terrorists to buy centrifuges, enriched uranium, plutonium, heavy water, missile warheads, dirty bombs." Petre took a deep breath. "Ceausescu and his gang of leader-friends have made a fortune."

"How did the Americans know this hidden, nuclear facility existed?" Dan asked, shaking his head in disbelief.

Petre answered by telling him the story of how it began.

"It all started with a black market trader in the Carpathians. He agreed to meet two strangers in the middle of the night at a ski lift in Transylvania. The two men were looking to buy something more dear than diamonds–a dirty bomb. They hoped the dirty bomb would lead them to its source, a nuclear site.

"'Do you know where to get one?' they had asked the trader.

"He led them to the basement of a small, smelly apartment. He put his flashlight next to a steel box the size of a can of sardines. He opened the box and showed them four small metallic lumps about six ounces each. 'Uranium-235,' he bragged. 'Makes a high explosive for a dirty bomb when it's packed with nuclear radioactive material. Only one lump like this, on the top of a missile, is needed to make a nuclear war head.'"

"Who were the two strangers?" Dan asked.

Petre didn't want to say that he had been one of them. He didn't answer.

"What did they do with the can?" Dan questioned.

"They bought it, so they'd have proof. Then they got the okay to search for the nuclear site. They found it in Transylvania, near the ski lift. That's where we're heading—to destroy it."

"Does Romania have the only nuclear institute like this one?"

"At the moment, there are five in the world. First, one in the States, in Los Alamos, New Mexico. In 1942, Robert Oppenheimer, physicist, worked there on the Manhattan Project and produced the first atom bombs, which were detonated on Hiroshima and Nagasaki.

"Number two's in Pakistan, under the eye of the 'father of the atom bomb,' Dr. Khan, with Ali Bhutto's money and blessings."

"Dr. Khan," Dan interrupted. "Didn't he mastermind the largest, illegal nuclear proliferation ring in history, and sell his centrifuges to Iran, Libya, North Korea, and now Turkey?"

"Yes," Petre replied. "Not many people know this, especially about Turkey."

"Dr. Khan's centrifuges would allow Turkey to build up their nuclear arsenal."

"Yes," Petre said. "But let's go back the locations of the other nuclear institutes.

"Then another one, right here," Petre said, pointing around him. "In the middle of Transylvania, where Ceausescu has created his dream lab, so he could prove he's the most powerful leader of all—and the richest. He once said, 'I may be short, but when I stand on my wallet, I'm the tallest one in any group.'"

Petre was disgusted, but his anger made him think of his life's work, and he shared his vision with Dan.

"American agents have to stop these nuclear bazaars from turning into nuclear freeways for smugglers transporting their parts to North Korea, Syria, Iraq, Iran, and Turkey."

Petre thought of his father; how he had died because of his radioactivated office while he tried to expose the truth to the world about Romanian communists and their nuclear activity. Petre's life mission was to put a stop to Ceausescu's nuclear program, so no one would be killed the way his father had been. It was personal for Petre: his responsibility, his motive, and his revenge.

Dan interrupted Petre's thoughts. "Is that the building in the distance?"

"Yes, the nuclear institute." Then they heard a sound, like a baby's cry. "Wolves." Taking out his radio, Petre communicated with his men at the foot of the mountain. "We've arrived. Move all the jeeps behind us and back us up with artillery once I give you the signal."

He indicated to Dan that they should take the side road on the left. "There's a hidden trail there that leads to the institute."

The small green jeep inched its way toward the modern building. Then the jeep, hitting a rock, stopped. The path was covered with huge boulders blocking the vehicle's passage.

"Impossible to get through," Dan said. "Better to walk. It'll be quieter."

Petre radioed his men to stop their cars until his next communication. He got out of the jeep and took a long stick from the backseat with an unusual apparatus at its base that served to defuse landmines. Then he slipped a heavy insulated sleeve on his right arm and shoulder. He took several hand grenades from a box and put them in his pockets.

Petre and Dan moved cautiously. Petre led with his stick, searching for landmines under rocks or buried in the ground. Feeling slightly nervous, but also eager, Petre climbed the hill first, barely making a sound until he saw the institute fifty yards in front of him.

He observed a guard on the left side of the building and another one on the right. He took off his insulated sleeve and signaled to Dan which guard each one of them should shoot. They twisted the silencers on their rifles and as Petre nodded, they each shot a guard dead.

Bingo, Petre thought, remembering how proud he felt during target practice when he got a bullseye.

He turned to Dan. "I'm going inside. Based on a new technology to detect ground markings of human activity, I know where the centrifuges and reactors are." Then he patted his Lieutenant on the shoulder. "You wait for me here outside."

"No," Dan insisted. "I'm going with you."

Petre's CIA operative chief in Virginia had advised him that it was always more prudent to work in pairs when there was a risk of ambush, so he allowed Dan to follow him. They crawled from the building's roof to a fire escape.

"Listen," Dan said. "Sounds. Animals."

"Bears or wolves?"

"Which is worse?"

"Both are bad," Petre warned him. "Ceausescu populated the area with brown bears so he could go hunting. He didn't care they'd come into town scavenging for food, making dogs and sheep their prey–even babies."

These sounds are from wolves. Petre saw a wolf jump from a large boulder onto the roof. Its two front legs were extended straight. It was ready to attack. As it jumped into the air, Petre fired. Then another wolf started howling, and then another and another. Petre and Dan shot each wolf until the area was quiet.

They continued down a ladder next to the fire escape. Once inside the building, he told Dan to stand guard until he returned.

Petre left to examine the series of rooms. He knew every detail of the facility from architectural plans and photos he had studied during the summer in Budapest with CIA operatives. They had also used a new type of satellite imagery known as synthetic-operating radar. By firing radio waves and measuring their echo, the satellite revealed more details than a photograph. It could even detect dirt kicked around by someone, or car tracks.

Now, as Petre was implementing all that he had learned, he felt exhilarated—the moment had come after years of planning. He would conquer his Scylla and Charybdis, two irresistible monsters —the training camp and the nuclear facility. He had the green light and talented fighters with him to do it.

Petre entered a room holding a special vacuum suction system, then he entered another room that contained an intricate water cascade. Next, he opened the door of a laboratory that contained a series of pressure machines, all hooked up to a master centrifuge that had special hollow tube rotors that could spin at an ultra-high speed of 70,000 rpm and enrich natural uranium into bomb fuel.

He stared amazed at the machines. The Western world had never realized an underdeveloped country like Romania could succeed in mastering such an intricate system of technology. The institute was designed to be Ceausescu's legacy.

Petre returned to Dan and they followed a strip of tiny green lights on the floor that led to the main reactor. The installation was built on two levels. On the upper floor were several security guards, armed with rifles to protect the scientists and machines below. On the lower level, Petre saw three men dressed in heavy white coats. From photos he had studied, he recognized the Russian scientist Lev Olinkoff, the Romanian physicist Vlad Lupovescu, and the Palestinian engineer Mohamad Haddad.

Petre whispered to Dan, "These are the key people who control this facility. They're working earlier than usual." He was concerned that they had been alerted and were preparing to destroy equipment.

"Have our men use smoke grenades immediately. I don't want fire where there might be nuclear material and machines," Peter said.

Dan spoke into his radio and gave the orders: "Cut down the power lines now." The main generator had to be destroyed to cut off the electricity. They couldn't risk sparks or fire.

The men were too far away and couldn't implement the orders, so the electricity remained on. Alarms bellowed throughout the facility. Dozens of security guards ran into the reactor room. Petre's men arrived and started shooting the guards. There was pandemonium—people running everywhere, shouting.

Petre and Dan fled, climbing down a ladder that led to a secret exit that Petre knew from the blueprints he'd studied. His men surrounded the institute and prevented the scientists from leaving. Petre gave the order. "Tie up the scientists. We'll turn them over to the Americans to interrogate."

Petre hadn't finished and didn't want to leave. "I know where the control machines are," he told Dan. "I'll radio the engineers to dismantle them."

Petre finished talking on his hand radio and turned to Dan. "Let's go, fast. There's more to do."

Fighting continued in Timisoara. Petre set up the Reverend's house as headquarters. From there, he worked with his Special Forces team–twelve selected soldiers, trained in different skills. At night, when most of his men were asleep, he went to the hospital to help as a doctor. The vials of penicillin and tetracycline that he had brought with him from his underground clinic were now of utmost importance.

For the next few days, he was in constant contact with CIA operatives and Gorbachev's aides. He wanted everyone to work with him and support the revolution. He had proven himself, and didn't want anyone *not* to follow him.

From Mokess's house, Petre met with leaders from other Romanian cities to thwart their discontent and consider their demands. He kept in contact with Ileyesco and together they reviewed plans for the final coup d'état in Bucharest.

Offering solidarity to the Romanian revolutionaries were neighbors from surrounding countries who had traveled far to help. Ukrainian doctors and nurses brought medical supplies. Serbian priests handed out bread and cheese. Moldovan farmers distributed food.

Crowds kept coming to do whatever they could. They all shouted for hope. In Budapest, Hungarians marched on the Corso Promenade holding candles to pray.

Everyone in Central and Eastern Europe remembered victory from the months before. In August, the Poles rebelled first. By electing Walesa and Mazowiecki their movement of Solidarity served as a model. The dominoes started to fall. On October 6, 1989, the Hungarian Socialist Party of Workers voted to abolish socialism and Karoly Grosz ousted Janos Kadar. On November 9, after twenty-eight years, the Berlin Wall crumbled to dust. In Bulgaria, on December 13, the communist Todor Jivkov was voted out. A week later, in Czechoslovakia, Vaclav Havel, the poet-leader, held a flaming torch as he led his people through a tunnel of darkness to freedom.

At the same time, revolution was burning in Romania. It was the only bloody uprising of all of them.

18

BUCHAREST, ROMANIA

December 21-23,1989

CEAUSESCU, the president of the Socialist Republic of Romania for the past twenty-four years, spoke from the balcony of Bucharest's Central Party headquarters.

"C-Comrades. B-Brothers..."

On this day after his visit to Iran, he had begun to stutter even more. He was nervous, thinking of the $1 billion dollars in gold bars and gold coins that he had deposited in the Bank of Tehran. If something happened to him, what would happen to his gold? Who would claim it?

"W-We will do all we can to d-defend our p-people." Nicolae Ceausescu raised his arms and turned to the crowd of hundreds of people. Smiling, he waited for their usual applause. Instead, there was a pause. Then, there was a rumble of catcalls rolled through Palace Square.

The chant *"TI-MI-SOA-RA"* suffused the air.

Ceausescu moved back. He almost fell. His wife, Elena, propped him up.

"Nicky, promise them something, anything."

"C-Comrades, b-b-rothers," he stammered, and his right leg fluttered with a frantic effort to stop his stutter.

"As of t-today, all workers will have a t-two thousand lei increase in their monthly wage."

The placation of two dollars extra a month only made the crowd angrier. Boos and hisses started faintly and then grew louder. The dictator was stunned. Never before had the people turned against him. His small body appeared minuscule as he hid behind his wife. Television cameras had been scheduled to film the rally live and they continued filming as the dictator showed a crumbling face to the country.

A young man climbed a tree and jumped onto the balcony. He raised his fist in front of Ceausescu and cried, "Swine! Thief! What were you doing in Iran these past few days? Putting our money into your secret account? We've been starving while you got rich."

An Iranian Revolutionary Guard next to Ceausescu threw the demonstrator off the balcony.

The mob yelled, "That's enough!"

Heavily armed commando forces surrounded the protesters and began firing. An armored car moved into the square and ran over two students. Iranian soldiers surrounded the crowd and beat people with wooden clubs. No army could prevent the tide of hatred that surrounded the dictator's platform. The people had had enough.

The next day, December 22, 1989, the rebellion had spread to all cities in Romania. Ceausescu made another attempt to address the crowd that had gathered in front of the Central Committee building in Bucharest's Palace Square, but the people threw stones at him. Ceausescu and his wife managed to escape to the balcony of the building and within seconds, a helicopter landed on the roof. Ceausescu, with his wife and two bodyguards, got inside, thinking the helicopter had been called to protect them from the violence of the mob.

The helicopter lifted them off the roof and landed in Targoviste, a medieval town 75 kilometers northwest of Bucharest. The bodyguards pushed the couple into a car. As Ceausescu tried to close the door, his suitcase opened, and gold coins fell to the ground.

Before the dictator and his wife could pick up the gold, five farmers stopped them with pitch forks, grabbed the suitcase, and buried the gold coins in their hay. The Ceausescus were rescued by so-called loyal friends, Ileyesco and General Stamkulesco, whom they trusted to help them.

Naïvely, they followed them to the army barracks.

The next day, at the same time as the previous day and in the same square, Ian Ileyesco, surrounded by Gorbachev's men, stood on the same balcony of party headquarters in Bucharest to announce that the Romanian Army had officially taken control of the country in a coup d'état.

"Comrades, brothers," he shouted. "Down with communism!"

Jubilation surged through the mob. Hundreds of people climbed on abandoned tanks and screamed, "Long live freedom!"

Ileyesco raised his arms for silence. The people stopped shouting.

"Fellow citizens, we will set up a new government and call it the National Salvation Front."

Everyone cheered. They waved their banners and signs.

He continued. "Our immediate task is to restore order. We will bring the dictator to a public trial."

Then from nowhere, one voice in the crowd pierced through. "Who is our leader?"

"I am!" Ileyesco responded and raised his fist to the crowd. "I will lead you to great heights."

The voice of that man came again, this time more meekly. "I heard our leader is a doctor. He started the revolution in Timisoara."

Ileyesco moved forward like a soldier ready to attack. "He's not in Bucharest. The people from Bucharest, not Timisoara, will lead Romania! I am here in your city as your leader." He raised his arms again.

Applause filled the streets of Palace Square. The people looked to the same stage from where, the day before, Ceausescu had been jeered. Today, they cheered the voice of promise.

A journalist from the newspaper *Scanteia* climbed onto the balcony next to Ileyesco and said that for the first time in forty years the Romanian people would read the truth in a newspaper.

A television broadcaster joined them and said that *Agerpres,* the Romanian news agency, no longer needed special approval to show TV programs.

The thrill of speaking freely and expressing their opinions openly suddenly overtook all the Romanian people. Church bells rang. car horns sounded throughout the city, and hidden speakers played Western music. The crowd started singing their national anthem and then changed their tune to *Olé Olé,* as if at a soccer match.

19

NEW YORK CITY

December 24, 1989

FOR THE PAST WEEK, Anca and Sandra had been secretly working at the United States Mission to collect aid and relief for Romania. Anca was hiding with Sandra—she didn't want anyone to know she was still in New York. Her colleagues at the hospital believed she was on vacation. Many of her Romanian friends thought she was in Paris helping Cristina prepare for the wedding. Actually, Anca was waiting to finalize her travel plans.

Until the details were synchronized with Washington, she was living with her daughter in an apartment near the United Nations that was owned by Paul, her director at Voice of America. It was the day before Christmas. No one was working in the U.S. Mission except Anca and Sandra, who were about to take a break to drive to Princeton for the Ivies' fencing tournament.

They left from a side door at First Avenue and 45th Street to get their car. Sandra was pulling a huge suitcase on wheels that was filled with three heavy fencing foils, two masks, sneakers, fencing knickers, and a Walkman with tapes. Once at the garage, they loaded the gear into their Volvo station wagon and drove to Princeton.

They talked in the car as they always had, from the time that Sandra was ten years old and Anca drove her to fencing tournaments and lessons. They'd talk about anything and everything. Sandra would chat about her classes, fencing practice, her friends, her father, and their vacations. Anca would discuss medicine, politics, literature, or movies—all the things she loved. Sandra would listen, asking her mother questions and wanting to learn. These were precious moments for Anca, who many times would drive slower so she could hold on to her daughter for a few minutes longer.

"You're lucky, Mom," Sandra said as she lowered the volume of her Walkman. "You've had such close friends all your life–Cristina, Mica, and Marina."

Anca smiled, remembering their friendship from the time they were thirteen years old. What they liked to do the most together was hike. Sundays, in any weather, was their time to feel free, wandering in the woods of Transylvania and the Carpathian Mountains. They'd walk through pine forests and valleys carpeted with purple heather. Their favorite game was to hold hands like a human chain. *"One for all and all for one,"* they'd sing, walking in a line and chanting their motto: *"We are the poets of our lives."* They'd bend down low, swing their arms to the sky and start again, holding hands, walking in a line, feeling free.

"The Four Musketeers." Anca sang their motto: *"We are the poets of our lives."*

"What does that really mean?"

"We vowed to create our own destiny—define our existence by our choices."

"Sounds like you all did just that: you, medicine; Cristina, design; Mica, choreography; and Marina, business."

"In a way, we were lucky we came from a communist country.

What a paradox, we were educated in a country that had no freedom, and yet, we had the greatest freedom of all."

"What do you mean?"

"We had gender freedom. Women and men were treated as equals. We were educated and encouraged to achieve equally alongside our male counterparts, and in any field we chose. In this way, we learned to compete and develop strong egos. One might say we were ahead of the times. We were independent before Western women were, who had to fight so much harder and longer than we did."

"And you all succeeded." Sandra commented, admiringly.

"Well, what is success?" Anca said, and then laughed. She then answered herself. "Success is ongoing. You always have to recreate your goals, as life changes you. Most of all, to be a success, you need balance, professional and personal, the mind and heart, a healthy body and strong soul. That brings happiness."

Sandra laughed. "Mom, you're really a doctor."

"No, I'm a woman."

"Is that why you're returning to Romania?"

"Yes—*un cri de coeur.*"

"I learned that in French class: a cry from the heart, a call of awakening."

"I see it as my reason for returning," Anca confessed in a tone that was not as light as her earlier banter. She put her arm around her daughter and told her, "You know, I never stopped loving your father."

Anca paused. She had just told her daughter a truth that she had never admitted to herself.

Then Anca's thoughts focused on her return to Romania, to the people she hoped would be there for her when she set off in two days. She hoped they'd protect her, just as she believed Alec's friends were watching over her and Sandi right now.

Sandra was thinking of her father. She had heard at the U.S.

Mission that the revolution had been a success. The leader was being pursued and had to escape for his life. "How did you know Dad would have problems before they happened? What told you that he'd have to escape?"

"Hard to explain. A phone call, friends talking, clues, and warnings. I felt danger inside me. Perhaps there's an animal instinct in us, like with turtles or snails. Must be the senses and our instinct to survive and to protect."

"Do you know where Dad is?" Sandra's tone was tense.

"Not exactly."

"How will you find him?"

"I'm sure there'll be a way once I arrive at the airport in Bucharest." She patted her daughter's hand to reassure her. "You know, in a communist country, it's hard to plan from one day to the next. People don't tell you beforehand what they'll do, and events don't necessarily go in a straight line. Even if it seems as if they're making it up as it happens, there's a logic underneath."

"I hope you haven't forgotten how they think. I hope Dad is safe. That man who came yesterday from Washington, Steven, did he visit you because of the relief fund or because of my father?"

"I'll tell you the truth because in a couple of days, you'll be on your own." She hoped her words weren't a prophecy.

Sandra moved closer to her mother.

"He gave me an American passport for your father and some microdiscs."

At the mention of microdiscs, Sandra tried not to appear surprised. "Does my father work for the CIA?" She couldn't suppress the thrill she felt at the thought. It seemed like the coolest thing in the world that her father was actually Dr. Spy.

"I don't know."

But Anca did know. She had known for years. Once she had arrived in Vienna and Petre's colleagues arranged her life—she knew. Yet she couldn't divulge this to Sandra. It was top secret, and she didn't want to worry her.

Instead, she answered, "I think the American government has been helping him. To what degree, I'm not sure."

Sandra remembered her last vacation with her father. The fleeting image of Budapest and the Corso Promenade passed before her eyes. She recalled him saying, "Of course I came. I was worried you weren't safe."

Anca interrupted Sandra's thoughts. "The man from Washington said it's important that I give your father some information." She took a deep breath. "I'm glad I have a tangible excuse to return to Romania after nineteen years."

Anca tried to smile, but instead, she said a silent prayer that she wasn't walking into a trap.

They arrived in Princeton, driving toward the campus from Route 1. Anca was happy to think about something other than Romania and its revolution, and turned her attention to the college's entrance, lined with tall maple and oak trees. Their branches formed an arch as the car passed through.

"We're entering paradise," Sandra marveled, opening her window. "I know this campus pretty well. I've fenced so many times here. The football field is on the left. Baseball on the right. Tigers! Rah! Rah!" she yelled, laughing. I don't know which I like better, Princeton or Yale. Something is different here."

Crossing the bridge, Sandra continued as tour guide. "That's the boathouse and lake. Look, the team is rowing, even in December. There's Jadwin Gym, where we're fencing. I can't get enough of fencing. *En garde.*" She snapped open her seat belt. *"Allez!"* she yelled and practiced a lunge and attack with her arm and hand.

Anca laughed, amused. "We're a few minutes early, so I'll look for a space." She entered Washington Road and made a left onto Prospect Avenue.

"That's where the eating clubs are. Look, on the right."

Anca drove slowly to admire the stone mansions, noticing that the ivy on the Gothic facades was still green despite some snow.

"There's Cap and Gown, another eating club," Sandra explained. "It's the house with the balconies. We've had lots of parties there, and lots of beer."

Anca continued driving, entering the center of town. Sandra pointed to an empty space on Nassau Street. As they got out of the car, a group of students wearing sweat clothes with large orange *P's* on the back of their jackets ran past them. Anca smiled and felt transported to a magical world where privileged youth in America reigned freely. It was an experience that Anca had never had, and she was happy that Sandra could know it.

"Let's take the side path," Sandra pointed. "I'll show you something special."

Tall evergreens as plush as those in Transylvania led them to an enormous garden. Dozens of herb bushes perfumed the air. Sandra picked a mint leaf from a bush and wiggled it in front of her mother's nose.

A clock chimed ten times. "Aha, I turn into a fencer. I can't wait. Let's go to Jadwin."

Anca and Sandra separated at the gym, Sandra going to the locker room and Anca to the stands. Seeing Mica wave to her, she walked toward her friend.

"Where's André?" Anca asked, kissing Mica on both cheeks.

"On rounds at the hospital. He'll come later to watch the twins fence in the afternoon for Men's Saber. I came earlier to see you and cheer Sandi."

"Thanks," Anca answered. She noticed Mica seemed tense, as if she wanted to say more, but hesitated. Anca diplomatically chatted of other things.

After a short time of preliminary fencing bouts, the final for the Women's Foil event was to begin, with Sandra fencing for Yale, and Ellen, a sophomore, fencing for Princeton. Anca was nervous watching, but tried to control her emotions. Mica, however, didn't care if people stared at her when she yelled.

The two girls went to the strip, each one in her corner, and attached their body cord from under their jacket to the round metal apparatus on the floor. Sandra then raised her foil to salute her opponent. Unexpectedly, she closed her eyes for several seconds.

Anca noted her daughter's intense expression, indicating she had left everyone and everything behind her for the moment. Sandra was entering a zone where she was seeing what she had to do for this bout: her timing and rhythm, how her arms, shoulders, knees, and legs should move. She left nothing to chance, attempting perfect execution. She was envisioning where to direct her artistry and skill, every move she had practiced over and over, year after year, so that her moves and passion would go straight to the target.

Crouching forward on the bench, Anca abandoned herself to the pleasure of admiring her daughter's precision and speed. "Come on, Sandi!" she screamed, and then smiled at Mica as she, too, set her feelings free.

Anca studied her daughter's attack strategy. She immediately established herself as the aggressor. She struck first, and then quickly retreated, switched to defense and waited, confusing her opponent.

Sandra's torso was protected by a vest made of a special lamé material. It was wired to an electrical apparatus on the ground that moved with her as she fenced. Her foil was also wired to a body cord that was clipped on inside her vest. In this way, when Sandra struck her opponent's vest at the target area, she created a complete electrical circuit that caused a green light to register her hit.

"Halt! Touch right," the referee announced. "Yale two, Princeton zero," the referee shouted.

The girls returned to the middle of the strip to start again. Sandra adjusted her mask, bent her blade, flicked the foil in the air, nodded to the referee that she was ready, bent her knees into position, and pointed her foil.

Ellen pulled up her knee socks and more hesitantly got into position.

"Ready?" the referee asked, and pressed his stopwatch.

Sandra had the momentum. She moved forward, forcing Ellen to retreat again. Watching Sandi fence reminded Anca of Petre, who also used his willpower to achieve his target— the revolution and freedom for his people. Anca couldn't help but feel that Sandi, unleashed while fencing, wouldn't stop until she achieved what she wanted. Anca smiled, thinking *Sandi is her father's daughter.*

"Halt! Touch right. Yale three, Princeton zero," the referee shouted. "Ready? Fence!"

"Two more points and the championship is hers," Mica assured her friend. "I love the way she fences–she's like a ballerina and a chess master all in one."

"She fences with her heart," said Anca. "Her greatest strength is speed when she's attacking. Look how quick she is when she's advancing."

"Anca!" Mica shouted. "Stop talking. Look—so quick! Sandi got another touch. The score is four-zero."

"One more, Sandi," her mother yelled. "One more and it's yours."

Anca focused on Sandra's legs moving forward. In one second, the tip of Sandra's foil struck Ellen's chest. Sandra screamed and waved her sword in triumph, took off her mask and shook her opponent's hand.

"She won!" Anca yelled, and hugged her friend. Then she and Mica ran together to the strip to congratulate Sandi and help her disengage her body cord from the electrical apparatus on the floor.

"You were great," Mica yelled, kissing her. "I'm going to nickname you Lightning."

Sandra smiled, "I had a strategy from the beginning. I kept mixing up my moves, changing my attacks. I wanted to keep the pressure on her, confuse her. When there's danger, my guts tell me what to do. You know what I mean?"

Members of the Yale team ran over to Sandi. "What a beautiful bout—a final of five-nothing. You didn't give her a break. Amazing!"

Sandi smiled when she saw Brian coming toward her. The cut on his jaw was healing, but still noticeable.

"Brava, *ma chérie*," he congratulated her and kissed her on both cheeks. His wound rubbed her skin. Feeling sorry for him, she apologized again for what had happened.

"Nah, nothing at all," he said, smiling. "You can pay me back."

"Yes?"

"Introduce me to your mother."

While Sandra dressed and showered, Anca and Mica had time to chat. "Forgive me for not staying to watch the twins fence," Anca said.

"Why the rush? André will be here soon, and we can take the kids afterwards for a snack."

Anca said quietly. "I'm leaving in a couple of days for Romania. I need to prepare."

Mica wasn't surprised. "That's what I wanted to talk to you about at Marina's, but Alec interrupted us."

"I thought so." Anca's body stiffened. She was still hurt that her friends had not told her everything they had known.

"I tried to call you all week, but you didn't answer your page."

"It's all right. I know you kept me out of the loop because you wanted to protect me."

"I didn't want you to worry about Petre. I knew it would hurt you all over again to bring up the past."

"I understand."

"Are you flying directly to Bucharest?"

"No. They want me to mix up my itinerary."

Mica was concerned. "If you need any help, call me immediately. I'll take the first plane out."

"Thanks."

"Do you have a plan of action?"

"No."

"Who have you been coordinating with, in case I need to help?"

"I'll be watched." Anca avoided a direct answer, and then hesitated. "I hope by the right people." She took her friend's hand. "I'll tell you about it when we all meet in Paris at Cristina's wedding."

They remained silent until Mica assured her, "I'll call Sandi every day and have her at my place for dinner." Then they heard Sandi shout, "Mom, I'm ready. Wanna go?"

As they drove back into the city, Sandra relaxed and listened to her Walkman. The late afternoon sky was already darkening behind the skyscrapers. Snowflakes covered the sidewalks, and last-minute Christmas shoppers were rushing through the streets carrying presents. Christmas music and carols came from speakers in the stores. There was a calm in the city and a feeling of good will.

At a red light, Anca kissed Sandra on the cheek. "I've been thinking. How about if you stay in the apartment that Paul gave us until we meet in Paris? It's safer than our place."

Sandra hesitated, and then said, "Okay." She knew her mother was concerned about leaving her alone. "You know, Mom, you never told me how you first became interested in politics." Lately, Sandra was interested in everything about her mother's youth. In the past week, with Romania's revolution blazing, and mother and daughter working together at the U.S. Mission, Sandra was looking at her mother differently, more objectively, and admiring what she had achieved, alone.

"In 1965," Anca recalled, "I was eighteen years old when Ceausescu came into power. I guess just about your age. My father was a well-known engineer, teaching at the University until the government forced him to resign for not following the party line. He decided to set up a wireless decoding system in our basement and transmit information to the Americans about the new dictator. He communicated to the CIA with the help of Alec, who was at that time his most gifted student."

"You mean *our Alec?*"

"Yes, my guardian angel. Somehow, my father's last transmissions to the Americans were intercepted by the Romanian Securitate. They arrested him and sent him to a psychiatric hospital... He died there from torture. My mother couldn't live without him."

Anca took a deep breath. "When I lost my parents, my world fell apart. I became fully an adult at eighteen."

How hard Anca had tried to give Sandra the security she had lost so young!

"There's one thing I don't understand," Sandra said. "If your father was imprisoned by the communists, why did they let you study medicine? You must have been on their blacklist."

"You're right—theoretically. When my father was arrested, many of his friends got nervous and switched sides. Not Alec; he was still a student and always anti-communist. He became a big brother to me, but many of the others became communists overnight. A few of them felt guilty for doing that and remembered their respect for my father. One friend became the dean of the medical school in Cluj. He arranged for me to study and live there and to specialize in infectious diseases. It was a big favor. Yet after graduation, I couldn't find a job in Cluj because I wasn't a member of the Communist Youth Party. He couldn't help with that. I had to go to the countryside."

"That was your good luck," Sandra said.

"Yes. It was fate. Your father was in charge of the clinic."

Sandra smiled, and Anca joined her.

Several minutes later, Anca drove into the garage at 45th Street. Both a little tired, they walked slowly back to the U.S. Mission to continue packing medicines and other aid for Anca's trip. Sandra pulled her heavy fencing suitcase and her mother held the Ivy League trophy.

In that instant, Anca understood that no matter how difficult her life had been, Petre was right to have saved them both. Sandra was her gift from God.

20

TIMISOARA, ROMANIA

December 26,1989

"Petre," yelled a radical revolutionary. "You're being too soft. All secret police agents should be executed!"

"Get rid of every politician who worked with the communists," shouted another man. "You can't trust them. They'll stab you in the back."

"No, listen," Petre said, and raised his arms to the dozens of people attending the meeting at Central Committee Town Hall. "Enough hatred. Let's use our energy positively. Let's build up our country. This reign of terror has lasted twenty-four years too long."

Then came the voices of dissent.

"Where were you when we were in jail? You traveled abroad. You had a privileged life, working for Ceausescu."

Another one said, "For nineteen years you lived in the capital in a luxurious apartment. You had everything. You were protected. *Why?*"

"The reason you wanted Ceausescu killed was so you could take over," a miner said. "It was for yourself, not for us."

Petre felt the people who had supported him before were now turning against him.

"You're an opportunist," came a voice from a dark corner of the room.

"How can we trust you?" shouted another.

Petre looked around the room. The day before, the crowd had cheered him. Today they were accusing him.

"Come into the light!" Petre yelled, angry that the people were denigrating everything he had worked for. "I dare you to say that to my face."

The voice didn't answer; it just whispered to neighbors.

"How can we reconstruct our country if there's dissent?" Petre warned them. "I can't be your leader if you don't believe in me." He wanted the people to rally to his side and cheer for him.

Silence filled the large meeting room. The crowd waited. They sensed he was losing control. Petre was losing power.

A voice muttered, "He's setting us up. He wants to be another dictator."

"We don't need him."

"Get rid of him!" yelled the same people who days before had cheered.

"I am Romanian," Petre said, "and I stand for Romanians, not Russians, and not foreigners. I sacrificed my family for the goal we all share. Trust me and I will lead you to greatness that is worthy of our ancestry."

"He sounds like a politician!" a voice yelled.

"Stop!" shouted Dan, Petre's lieutenant, as he entered the noisy room. "I am privileged, like many of you, to have worked with such a hero. I was with him when he led us to destroy the terrorists' training camp. Then he cleared the path for a special team to wipe out the nuclear institute. Without his courage, this could not have happened."

The youngest man in the group came forward in agreement. "I'm the leader of the students in Timisoara. If you and your families are to see a better life, it's because of Petre. You should get on your knees and thank him."

The student's voice grew bolder. "You'll never have a more honest leader. Without him, our country will continue to be corrupt."

Another student raised his fist and shouted, "You shouldn't speak against Petre!"

"Why not?" argued a miner. "He's not the one who captured Ceausescu. I heard it was Ileyesco in Bucharest."

"Yes, Ileyesco!" shouted another miner. "He has contacts with Gorbachev. He'll get the Russians to invest in our country. Give us jobs!"

"How can you trust someone linked to the Soviets?" the student answered. "We need a democrat."

"A democrat? You mean someone paid by the Americans?"

Shouts of "*Boo!*" filled the room.

"Listen to me!" another student yelled. "It's Petre, no one else, who devised the plan to arrest Ceausescu and have him executed. Petre wasn't in Bucharest because he was here, in Timisoara, to protect all of you and to start the revolution from your city, where we have solidarity among ethnic groups. Where is your loyalty now?"

"Throw this child out!" roared the miner who several days earlier had marched alongside the students. "Someone must have given him lunch to get him to say that."

"No," came a voice from the door. "Leave the boy alone."

Mihai Strancusi stormed into the room. "Who's behind this mutiny? You saw with your own eyes how Petre led you to victory."

"No!" insisted one of the dissenters. "He wants to be the next dictator."

"Freedom without direction results in chaos," said the priest. "We need a leader to assure order. A stabilizing force—an educated man."

"You can't be trusted either," yelled the same man who, days before, had worked with the man of God.

"Stop fighting! I want to help," said Petre calmly as he raised his hands. "I want this country to move beyond violence. The Iron Curtain has been lifted. Now is the time to build democracy."

"He's not thinking of our future. He's thinking about his own," shouted the miner.

Petre turned his back to the crowd. He was disgusted that they weren't trusting him to lead the next stage of government. "I'm leaving." His voice lost its confidence. "Ceausescu is dead, but Romania's story is not over. There will be more horrors."

The priest tried to stop him. "Stay, Petre. Don't walk out now. Fight for your leadership. The people need you."

"No. They're not ready."

"If you retreat now, Ileyesco will stay in power. He's not the right man to lead."

"I can't force the mob to back me."

"If you try to leave, they'll kill you," the priest warned his friend.

Petre moved toward the door. He shoved his fists deep in his pockets. "I'll take the risk."

"No, you have to escape," the priest advised. "I'll go with you."

Petre didn't answer. Instead, he walked alone through the dark, empty corridors of Party Hall. At the door, he noticed a mirror. He remembered how Ceausescu had ordered a mirror to be placed next to every door in every Central Committee hall in every village. The dictator wanted to make sure his hat was on straight before he greeted the crowds.

Petre stopped in front of the same mirror. From the reflection, he saw his sarcastic smile. He studied his tired face, the wrinkles on his brow, the beginning of a beard lined with gray, the dark pouches under his eyes. He didn't recognize himself.

He stared harder at the image. He thought he detected the ambition for power fill his face. Power was a drug, no different than an intoxicating fruit from a sweet lotus, similar to what prevented Odysseus and his men from returning home.

"What am I doing here?" he asked the reflection. "I led my men to destroy a dictator, destroy his training camp of terrorists, and destroy his nuclear network. The people should be grateful to me."

He walked out the door toward the setting sun. Images of revolution filled his eyes. He saw before him the people cheering while the dictator's statue was brought crashing down. He could almost smell the burning candles of celebration and victory, but then he saw reality. "How can I change their readiness to switch sides, or their believing false statements filled with lies?"

He walked faster and dug his boots into the snow. He felt resentful and filled with anger that he had sacrificed more than twenty years of his life and had given up his wife and daughter for an ideal.

"How ironic. I engineered the revolution, inflamed the people, and now they want to get rid of me. Is it possible they would actually kill me?"

As Petre walked away, the cracked sidewalk appeared before his eyes like a broken ladder that had fallen down.

He had dared to climb too high.

21

NEW YORK CITY

December 26,1989

IT IS NOT easy to go home after nineteen years away.

Two weeks before, when Anca had a premonition that something was happening in Romania and that Petre was at the center of the revolution, she had telephoned the CIA agent, Steven Bradley, who had helped her years before in Vienna. It took her three days to reach him in Washington because his phone was constantly busy. When she heard his voice, she was relieved to know he was still working there.

"Something in me feels that Petre will be in danger," she told him. "I can't analyze this feeling, but it's inside me, and I'd like to help."

At first, Steven prevaricated, saying he didn't know anything about trouble in Romania. He wasn't sure where Petre was, and he couldn't say if Petre was or would be in danger. She understood from his hesitations that he knew every detail about the Romanian revolution and its leader, even from his soft leather chair. At the end of the conversation, Steven said he'd have to verify the situation.

Several days later, he called her with a plan. She could help get Petre out of Romania. He suggested she fly to Bucharest, where he would arrange a car and driver for her, as well as a safe house and trusted people with whom she could stay in the countryside. He would oversee every detail of the plan.

———

Before Anca could leave New York, there were many obstacles she had to overcome. She had to be careful about being seen in the city while she was hiding at the U.S. Mission. Anca was also reticent to leave her daughter alone in New York even though Alec had notified U.N. security guards to patrol the U.S. Mission and keep an eye on Sandra.

Anca decided to tell Mark the truth about her trip.

"Don't go," he said to her. "The communists are still there. They'll find out you're the ex-wife of the head revolutionary. You're not safe. Don't you think they know you escaped illegally?"

The doctor in him was pragmatic, and correct in his diagnosis, but she knew the man in him was jealous. She understood he feared that if she returned to Romania, she would never return to him.

Anca felt guilty about hurting Mark. She wanted to be kind, to reassure him that she was just leaving for a few weeks and would come back to New York. She couldn't come out and say that she'd return to him.

Mark knew she was suffering with conflicting emotions, and he felt sorry for her. He was always ready to forgive her and help.

Meanwhile, Petre was nowhere to be found. After Anca spent the day on the phone with Steven and his colleagues, they tried to locate him. When Petre had walked out of the meeting room in Timisoara, he had left the city. Some operatives in Vienna thought the Romanian secret police had killed him, but Steven stood firm that he was alive.

In fact, when all Timisoara was asleep, Petre had escaped with Mokess and his family and the priest. The small group hid during the day in convents and monasteries and traveled at night on skis through the mountains, heading toward the Hungarian border.

Petre, Mokess, and the priest could not communicate directly with their colleagues in Washington, but there were secret operatives in Transylvania and Budapest who were surveying the situation and keeping Washington informed.

For Anca, the logistics of traveling had its complications. Tarom, Romanian's national airline, had discontinued all flights. They were using the few planes they had to ship medicines and donations to Romania from the U.S. and Europe.

In addition, Steven didn't want her to fly directly to Bucharest. "Too conspicuous," he said. Instead, he arranged that she'd take a minor service to Dublin, then another one to Lisbon, then Barcelona, and then Geneva to join the group Doctors Without Borders.

As Anca traveled with them eastward, she had to remind herself that she was just a doctor who volunteered to help Romanians wounded and involved in the revolution.

PART IV

RETURN HOME

DECEMBER 27-28,1989

Odysseus and His Crew

22

ROMANIA

December 27-28,1989

ANCA MOVED SLOWLY through the long customs line at Bucharest's Otopeni International Airport. She followed the Romanian sign that said *PASAPORT*.

"*Buna dimineata*. Good morning," Anca said to the customs officer as she felt his eyes study her fur hat, her leather suitcase, and her black doctor's bag. Trying to be nonchalant, she handed him her American passport and the return half of her plane ticket.

"Doctor, *hmm*," he mumbled. "*Pasaport* American. *Hmm*."

Anca held her breath. She wanted no long conversation in Romanian, and no complications.

"*Nascuta in Spera*. Born in Spera," he said, inspecting every page of her passport, even the blank ones. Then he opened her plane ticket. "*Médecins Sans Frontières*."

"I'm part of a group of humanitarian doctors," she answered, holding up her doctor bag as if she needed to give visual proof. "We want to help."

He stared at her with unfriendly eyes. "Why do you want to help after all these years?"

She smiled, trying to hide the fact that she didn't like him.

"Where are you going?" he asked.

"Transylvania."

"Why? It's dangerous there for a woman alone." He surveyed her from head to toe, stopping at her breasts.

She buttoned her coat. "I'm a doctor. I speak Romanian, Hungarian, and English."

He wasn't impressed, so she played her trump card.

"I have a Christmas present for you." Anca took out a box of Swiss chocolates and a package of Nescafé.

He grabbed the gifts out of her hands and hid them under the counter. He returned her passport and plane ticket and waved her on.

Anca walked away slowly, looking for the way out. Noticing the four windows in the room were shattered, she glanced down, but she couldn't help but notice blood stains covering the floor. Broken glass and used bullet casings were scattered around the room. It looked like someone had tried to sweep up the remnants of war, but hadn't finished. There was one electric bulb for the entire room, and its 40 watts flickered. *Nothing has changed,* she thought.

The airport was empty except for several policemen carrying machine guns. Anca looked at them, smooth-skinned boys dressed up in war clothes. She felt sorry for them.

She finally found the door marked EXIT and walked through a room that had served as a morgue for the victims of the revolution.

A thin, youngish man, wearing his Sunday best, closed the door of his tiny blue Romanian Dacia, and walked toward the airport's main room.

"*Buna dimineata.*" He bowed at Anca and removed his woolen cap. "Dr. Rodescu?" he asked and bowed again. "My name is Mihai. Everyone calls me Micky. WDC sent me."

He didn't look up from the floor. He took her bags and stood respectfully a few feet behind her. Without moving his head, he eyed some people staring at them.

"Where are we going?" Anca realized she was now in the hands of WDC—Washington, D.C. She had looked inside for a public telephone to call Mark and tell him she had arrived safely, but there was none. Then she thought, *how naïve I am to think that a telephone exists.* Communism controlled everything personal–especially phone calls.

"We're driving to Dova, the town where you worked as a doctor."

"That makes sense." She felt better. "How are the roads?" she asked, squeezing into the car while surveying the parking lot. Everything looked gray: the cloudy sky, the buildings covered with bullet holes, the potholed roads, even the snow.

"Not bad. I can do it, despite the ice and snow. It's nothing for me."

Anca had known she'd have to be prepared for anything. She kept telling herself not to be nervous. The American government knew where she was going. Yet she feared they wouldn't be able to protect her if she was in danger. She was on her own.

Then she thought, *Who is this driver? Why was he the only driver at the airport?*

She realized she should have demanded some form of authentication. She had been satisfied too quickly when he said he had been sent by WDC.

"Do you have a license or identity card so I can see your full name?" she asked him.

He took out a photo driver's license and handed it to her in the backseat. *MIHAI GRIESCU,* she read. She wasn't completely reassured. *Why had the airport been empty? Apart from my airplane, why was there no air traffic?*

"Do you have a full tank of gas?" she asked, trying to make sure he was prepared for an emergency.

"Yes. I waited in line yesterday when I was told about my mission. I even got an extra ten liters." He took out the red plastic can to show her. She told herself to believe him, but still, she wanted to test him further.

"I'd like to pass through Sibiu and Cluj before we go toward the Hungarian border," she said with authority.

"It doesn't make sense to take that route. It'll take more time, maybe the whole day."

"I know, but I lived in both cities as a girl. I don't think I'll ever have the chance to see them again."

"The roads are bad through that section of the mountains. We'll lose a lot of time."

"That's fine. I still want to go to both." She wanted to use the detour as an excuse to make sure he wasn't a double agent working for the Romanian secret police. The detour would give her time to see if they were being followed.

"I want to see what has happened over the years," she said, hiding her true intention. She hoped she'd be able to sense after driving with him if he were truly tapped to protect her and not denounce her.

"Besides," she smiled, charmingly, "I have a Christmas present for you." She gave him a bag filled with bars of chocolate, cookies, and coffee. They both knew he expected a gift.

"America is wonderful, *da?*" he said, and took the bag as if they meant nothing to him.

"*Da.*" She removed her gloves while she looked out the rear window to see if anyone was following them. "America can be magical. For many people it's a chance to become someone else— to have a new name, a new job, and to start a new life."

"Is it true everyone owns a television, a stereo, a refrigerator, a car, and a big house?"

She smiled. "Not everyone, but if you wish, I'll tell you about America."

Anca opened the window. The smell of burning leaves filled the air. Dust from the airport had slowly been replaced by the aroma of charred herbs, leaves, and plants. People were burning whatever they could to stay warm.

She saw before her scenes that appeared both slightly foreign and also familiar as she tried to remember them from her youth. Transfixed, she focused on the moving figures as their car passed them by. People walked on the roads. There were no sidewalks. In the absence of strollers, mothers carried their babies in their arms. A young boy seated in an open wagon cuddled up to his father while his black eyes stared curiously at Anca in her passing car.

A small truck with a load of seltzer bottles passed them. She examined a scar on her hand from a bottle that had almost exploded in her face when she was a child.

She looked out the window as Micky put on the radio. In between the pine trees lining the road, she saw strips of farmland. In a field, a little boy dressed in red was running after a shepherd's dog. Hundreds of white dots painted the fields. As the car traveled on, the dots became sheep, and Anca saw the shepherd boy wave his wand at the herd. Farmers, bent over with hoes and pitchforks, stood up when they heard the car's engine rumble into second gear. Anca waved to them and marveled as dozens of haystacks pointed to the sky.

A church with a steeple made of steel reflected the morning sun. Anca remembered Sundays in church when her mother played the organ. She tried to recall the Bach fugues her mother had loved. Tears came to her eyes and ran down her cheeks as she thought about her mother and father. She started to sob and leaned her head out the window to muffle the sound.

Once in control, she studied the line of mountains, counting each tip to force herself to think of something else. Then she tried to concentrate on the sounds from the valley echoing with the splash of brooks and the roar of rivers. She hadn't thought she'd get so emotional.

Everything was different from what she remembered, and yet so much was the same. Scenes appeared to her as if she were seeing them for the first time—pastel churches with soaring steeples, pale yellow houses roofed with multi-colored terra cotta tiles. They all passed before her, the villages of Romania, a mosaic of color and history. This was her old world.

She sat back in her seat and returned to her memory's moving screen. As they drove, she kept seeing wagons on the road. All sizes and types were pulled by a single horse, or two oxen. They were driven by farmers, women, and youngsters. Eventually, there were more wagons on the road than cars. When Micky slowed down to pass one, she waved to the people and remembrance overtook her. She was no longer the outsider observing, no longer the Prodigal Daughter returning home. She swayed in the back seat of the car and the small vehicle became her shield, protecting her as she tried to absorb the present and find the past. This was the Romania of nineteen years ago, of hundreds of years ago. This was the Romania of the loved ones she had lost.

With each kilometer they traveled and each village they passed, her life in America moved farther away. The sight of small villages nestled high up in the mountains became more real than the skyscrapers of her Western world. Scenes from her youth broke through the restraints of memory and emerged from the shadow of time. She desperately wanted to touch the medieval houses, to walk through the town squares, and to follow the geometric stones of the steps leading to a world that hadn't changed. The cold wind against her face and the tall pine trees didn't allow her to come too near.

Micky stopped short, and Anca swayed in the backseat. She held on tightly as he announced, *"Sibiu."*

He turned off his music and asked her, "Do you want to stop here or go on to Cluj?"

"Let's stop here in Sibiu first."

Rows of medieval walls fortified the city. Houses stood no more than three or four stories tall. The tiled roofs sloped down steeply, and the windows looked like half-opened eyes winking in their slits. The windows were called the "eyes of Sibiu," and she felt them watching her as she tried to turn yesterday into today.

As they approached the main square, Anca marveled at the geometric beauty of the line of Baroque houses and buildings. She recalled Bruckenthal Palace's enormous library where she had read so many books, and next to it, the first hospital and pharmacy ever built in Romania. Before her was Sibiu's square, laced with wrought iron balconies, like a design only the gods could have made. It appeared as if the square's ground was created from stone blocks set out to welcome her home.

As Micky circled the square, Anca smelled incense. She noticed a statue of the Madonna at the base of a drinking well. Above the stone wall was a sign: "Those who drink from these waters will not be thirsty for a century."

Anca tried to remember if the water fountain had been built on top of a sacred base or if it was where a miracle had once taken place. Next to the well, a group of women was praying in front of the Madonna. They were holding the same candles that several days ago had lit the way for freedom.

"Stop the car," she said, getting out and walking to the well to drink its water. A toothless woman, dressed in black, gave Anca a candle. "*Pace*, Peace," she whispered and lit Anca's candle from her own.

They continued on, through the valleys of Transylvania toward Cluj. Anca saw street signs and names written with both Hungarian and Romanian spelling. It was the end of the day, and farmers were walking home. She noticed that one carried a shovel on his shoulder, another a sickle, another a hoe. The cows from the fields walked next to them on the road, and when the animals smelled their homes, they entered their respective yards, ringing their bells like honored guests.

As the sun was setting, a group of farmers in a field clustered together by a fire to eat dinner. Seated on the earth and using the last light of day, they shared their bread and cheese. Inside their huts, they knew, it would soon be dark.

Anca and Micky traveled on icy and snowy roads that reflected the crimson of the setting sun. Anca saw women wearing the same scarves on their head in the fashion of the old days. Men wore the same fur hats. The day's farm tools were strapped to the brackets above the wagon wheels, just like always. Farmers were chatting the same way their grandparents did years before them. The scene looked the same as nineteen years ago. Anca realized how much she had missed this world, how much she had loved it, and how much she still loved it now.

They approached Cluj at sunset. Anca marveled as the sun folded into the white mountains surrounding the medieval town. It appeared as if Cluj were on fire. The dramatic beginning of night's end filled her with remembrance.

She was going home, and memories of her youth filled her with an excitement she thought she had lost forever. The car climbed up Citadel Hill, and Anca asked Micky to stop. She got out of the car and took in the entire city so she could hold on to it forever. She found St. Michael's Cathedral and remembered the sound of its bell. She smiled as she eyed the group of bronze statues and iron horses in the square, powdered with fresh white snow.

Anca returned to the car and opened both windows. Outside nothing in Cluj had changed, but while the car traveled over the once familiar road, she wondered, how much had she changed?

"Dr. Rodescu," Micky said, interrupting her thoughts. He had left the main road because it had been blocked with snow drifts and he was trying to take another road, but it was icy. "It's getting dark. The road isn't lit. What do you want to do?"

Anca looked at the roofs of houses covered with snow. "Let's stop in Cluj for the night. We'll leave tomorrow morning." She needed time to think.

"Just what I thought, too."

"Do you know a place where we can stay?" she asked him, now feeling he was trustworthy.

"My sister lives nearby. We'll be safe there." Then he added, "I built the house myself."

Anca smiled, relieved. "It would be my honor to spend the night at your sister's home."

Her thoughts returned to the memory of mountains and she looked for traces of a ski slope.

"Wait, Anca. Don't struggle. I'll get your poles. They slipped down the slope."

"Petre, do you think I'll really learn to ski? I keep falling."

"Of course. You just started. Be patient."

"Don't help me. I want to do it all by myself."

Anca sat back in Micky's car. Her eyes moved up the slopes and searched for a T-bar or a tow rope. She prayed she'd find Petre there, just as he was years ago, pointing to the right trail.

"Over here. Follow me."

She wondered where Petre was, and how she could find him. *Can I trust these people who have been set up to guide me?*

"Dr. Rodescu, Dr. Rodescu." She heard Micky's voice as if from far away. "We're here."

23

TRANSYLVANIA, ROMANIA

December 28,1989

> *These riches are possessed, but not enjoyed.*
>
> — Homer, *The Odyssey*, Book 4

It was the soft mist of morning that Anca had missed most of all. The fragile vapor had a way of mysteriously spreading its drops from the mountains to the meadows. In the winter, the dew turned to fine particles of ice and all the fields were covered in a blanket of pink-white frost. Clouds were colored red by the morning sky, and blended with the pine trees in a crimson hue. She remembered how she'd start her day happy.

Anca and Micky had parted from his family at the same time as the roosters announced a new day. After much laughing and wishes for a good journey, Micky shrugged and said, "We need to go."

They traveled southwest from Cluj into the mountainous

region of Transylvania. Then after four hours of driving toward the Hungarian border, the land suddenly turned flat. Fields of wheat and grain replaced the hills and mountains. She remembered the times Petre had led her through these fields, looking for herbs and plants, and the day ended by making love in a bed of blue flowers.

Micky and Anca traveled over a narrow road that looked as if it had been carved out of fields of white snow. In the back seat, she wiped the frosty window. There were no houses, no animals, and no signs of life. There was just silent white, snow-filled fields. The car edged forward.

In the distance, Anca heard sounds of laughter. Music seemed to emerge from the snow as if spring were bursting through the cold. She recognized the pure melodic sound of the *naï*—a shepherd's wooden flute—a *flûte de Pan*.

Two black horses pulling a wooden wagon emerged from the white fields. Four men, dressed in black coats and black hats, stood tall in their wagon, stark and dark against the white background. Their black figures grew larger, and Anca saw one was playing the naï. Next to him was a flute player, and next to him an accordionist, and a guitarist. Their music came closer.

"Gypsies," shouted Micky. "I hope they don't steal my car." He hid the bag of chocolates, cookies, and coffee under his seat.

"Don't be ridiculous," Anca said. "The tallest one is carrying a bouquet of pine and spruce branches."

Reluctantly, Micky stopped. Anca opened her window.

"Buna dimineata," said one of the men, and he jumped off the wagon. He handed Anca the bouquet and bowed deeply.

She smiled. *"Merçi multumesc."*

Suddenly, the three other black figures jumped off the wagon, ran toward Anca's opened window, and greeted her with Gypsy music.

The youngest one raised his *naï* and played a melody that

sounded like a trot of horses' hoofs. The guitarist, standing next to him, made a motion with hands and moved his body as if he were a horse. He was pantomiming the song they were playing and pointed to her.

"*Cai*, horses," laughed Anca as she joined the game.

The lead musician nodded his head, "*Da*. Yes, traveling." Then he played another melody. It reminded Anca of birds in flight. The guitarist continued the charade, flapping his wings and whistling as the naï played on.

"*Pasari*, birds," shouted Anca and her green eyes sparkled.

"Yes. Going far away, like you."

Then the flute player lowered his head and played another melody. The accordionist pretended he was crying. It was a Gypsy love song about two lovers who part from one another. Anca remembered the words: *Te iubesc pe vesnicie.* I will love you forever.

She got out of the car, wanting to touch the wagon, to feel the past with her hands. She remembered when she had last heard the song, nineteen years ago. The Gypsies had given a party for her, thanking her for the lives she had saved. A young woman with eyes shaped like almonds and the color of black diamonds raised her baby to Anca and said, "Dr. Rodescu, it's because of you I have my son."

The tall Gypsy stopped playing his music, went back to his wagon, and returned to Anca with two small bottles of plum brandy. He opened them, handed one to Anca, and kept one for himself. He raised his bottle to Anca and bowed. "*Noroc si sanatate.* To your health."

Anca raised her bottle of *tsuica* to the group of Gypsies. "*Noroc.* To life."

"*Bine ati venit*, Welcome home, Dr. Rodescu," said the leader of the group.

Anca studied his face. "How do you know me?" She already

knew the answer as if it were written on his palm. He had the same black diamond eyes as her friend. Now she realized she was safe.

"You saved my life. My name is Tanase."

Anca smiled. "Is your mother still living in town?"

"Yes. She received word that you were coming to visit." He paused, not saying from whom she had received word. "That's how I knew you'd be on this road. It's the only one. My mother sent me to tell you she'll do everything to help you."

Anca nodded. Evdochia's phone call had been Anca's first clue that Petre was in trouble.

The violinist played another Gypsy song. Anca stretched her arms to the young man and they danced together in the snow. Then he picked her up and placed her in his wagon. The other musicians joined them. Tanase took a long stick, climbed up to the seat, and hit the horses. "Let's go," he shouted.

Anca waved goodbye to Micky. *"Merci. Merci."*

"Wait," he protested, upset at her decision to leave before his task was done. Micky had promised WDC to take Anca to the Gypsy camp, to Evdochia's house.

"It's all right," she assured him. "I know these men. They're friends."

He took her bags from his car and put them in the wagon. "Women," he mumbled to himself. Then he turned to Anca and said, "If you need me, let me tell you how to contact me."

But Anca and the Gypsies had already vanished into the white fields.

Micky stared at the black figures. Taking off his hat, he rubbed his bald head. "A doctor with Gypsies? How strange. What happened to her in America?"

Perched on top of the wagon, Anca looked around the center of town as they passed through. Men on horses and families in wagons stopped at the well from the Mures River to let their horses drink their fill. It was just as she remembered. Yet something was different. In the main square for the first time since Ceausescu had been dictator, there was a Christmas tree and Christmas carols chimed from speakers that days before had blasted lies and threats from the secret police.

The Romanian Orthodox church now had its doors wide open, and the smell of burning candles filled the crisp air. She remembered that years ago, there had been a church with the icon of Saint Irena who had cried real tears. She wondered whether the tears had stopped now that the people had finally found a certain peace.

Suddenly, a gust of wind blew across her face and reminded Anca that she wasn't dreaming. Her hat blew off, and Tanase stopped the wagon to chase it. She had forgotten how terribly cold winter in Transylvania could be.

"Tanase, where's your mother's house?" Anca was trying to get reoriented.

"Further down," and he pointed to distant fields.

Anca gave up looking for the medical clinic where she and Petre had once worked; she would find it later. Instead, she and Tanase continued traveling in the wagon, chatting.

"Tanase, does your mother work?" Anca asked.

"Yes. She begins her day at five o'clock. She takes this wagon and goes to several egg farms to load the wagon with eggs. Then, she continues on to convents and monasteries in the region and delivers her goods. At the end of her day, she goes to meetings."

Anca listened carefully, like a doctor listening to a patient's medical history, trying to put the pieces together. She realized the plan—two women delivering eggs.

As the carriage drove along on the icy path, Anca thought back to the time when Tanase had been an infant with typhus. She had visited mother and child every afternoon for three months. Not having a wagon, she'd walk and carry her black bag in one hand and a package of food in the other. It was then that she and Evdochia had become friends, talking together about so many subjects, long into the night. Anca remembered how angry the townsfolk had been. Patients used to bring her food in lieu of money, and they weren't happy to think she gave their food to Evdochia and her baby. They were even more surprised that Petre gave tetracycline to the Gypsies and not to communists.

Before Anca could ask another question, they arrived at the Gypsy town. Rows of small, wooden-framed huts with carved window shutters comprised a section of fifty houses. Evdochia's house was the first one in the first row and had a large garden in the front. Anca recalled that the location and garden marked a position of honor.

She noticed an unusually large Christmas wreath hanging on the front door, with two white pigeons made of straw. Tanase played with them, swinging them back and forth as he waited for his mother to greet them at the door. *He's like a big child,* thought Anca. She estimated that he was about a year older than her daughter.

"Dr. Rodescu, Dr. Rodescu, is it you?" called the Gypsy. *"Bine ati venit*—Welcome to my home." Evdochia bowed deeply and extended her arms to her guest, palms upward, in deep respect.

Anca held back her tears at seeing Evdochia after so many years. Uncomfortable that Evdochia had bowed, she raised her and said, smiling, "Don't bow. We're friends," and she kissed her solemnly on each cheek.

Tanase was surprised that the doctor made such a gesture, but he was also proud. "Mother," he said, "I'm going to make your deliveries today. Enjoy Dr. Rodescu's visit."

"Good idea," she said. "This will prepare the nuns for tomorrow. Make sure you give the eggs personally to each mother superior. Don't forget to go to all six convents and two monasteries at the Hungarian border. Tell everyone I have a nun from Moldova who's visiting me. That's why I'm not making deliveries today."

Anca laughed. Now she understood the specifics of the escape. Anca would disguise herself as a nun, and she'd join Evdochia tomorrow. No one would bother a nun visiting a convent. If someone spoke to Anca, Evdochia would say she only spoke Russian. The less said, the better.

"*La revedere Doamnelor.* Goodbye, ladies." Tanase wanted to kiss Anca's hand, Romanian style, but she took his hand instead and shook it, American style. She wanted to kiss his cheek as well, but she didn't want to embarrass him. He closed the door, smiling, and left the women alone.

"*Va rog.* Please, sit down. I'll put some wood on the fire."

Evdochia was wearing a beautifully embroidered skirt, the type that Gypsies don for special occasions. Her traditional white ruffled blouse was covered with a red and gold apron that extended to her ankles. The bottom of the skirt was decorated with long red, yellow, and blue fringes, Romania's national colors. Coins jingled at the hem. Evdochia appeared regal with her black, wavy hair, which she wore long and free. She gave an impression of strength.

As Anca took off her coat and hat, she watched Evdochia prepare the fireplace. She remembered their conversations in front of the fire years ago. They had opened up their hearts to each other and felt such a strong connection, despite their different backgrounds. Anca realized now what that thread of connection had been: the desire to do good. Anca, the doctor, and Evdochia, the matriarch of the Transylvanian Gypsies. Both wanted to help others have a better life. In their giving, they felt happy.

Anca studied Evdochia's face as the flames of the fire reflected on her skin: burning black eyes, high cheekbones, chiseled chin, long straight nose, and rich black hair without any gray. Her strong body hadn't aged. Only her hands revealed the passage of time. Rough and scarred, her fingers were disfigured. Thick veins showed through her olive skin, revealing a life of physical work. Anca became fixated on the sure movements of the strong fingers as Evdochia broke sticks and threw them into the flames, hardly feeling the fire.

Evdochia's house looked as if she and Tanase had made everything themselves. The windows were covered with red and white curtains of a geometric pattern. The wooden dining table of pine was hand carved, and each wooden chair had a different sculpted design. The floor was made of plain pine planks, thick and warm to the eye, and the wooden couch had cushions made of the same red fabric as the curtains. A red area rug covered the pine floor. Even the dishes were made from a soft pine.

"Let's have something to eat." Evdochia pointed to the table that was set for two.

Anca remembered she only had tea for breakfast. She had been embarrassed to ask Micky's sister for anything more; their empty cupboard looked so poor. "I'm actually quite hungry," she said and warmed her hands first at the fireplace. Then she sat down.

"Would you like some bread and cheese? I even made a cherry soup for you. I remember how much you liked it."

Anca smiled. "The last time I had cherry soup was with you."

"Would you like some herbal tea, also?"

"You have some?"

"Sure, I knew you were coming." Evdochia took several green herbs from a box, tore the leaves into small pieces, and mixed them with shavings of a flower in a pot of boiling water. Anca breathed in the vapors. The perfume took her back to the fields of blue flowers where she and Petre made love.

"Dr. Rodescu," Evdochia interrupted. "Do you want more soup? More tea?"

"I didn't realize I had finished them both. I feel stronger already." Then Anca laughed, remembering Evdochia's talent of fortune telling. "Before you ask me if I want you to read my fortune from my tea leaves, I must remind you that you already did see the future. Your phone call said it all. I listened. I'm here."

Evdochia smiled, pleased.

Anca stood up, went to warm her hands at the fireplace again, and asked, "Are you working with Petre's friends in Washington?"

Evdochia didn't answer, but nodded.

"Always? Since I've known you?"

She nodded again and smiled. "Let's talk of other things."

"Okay."

Evdochia poured her another cup of tea.

"I wonder if time has touched you here at all," Anca said, looking around her friend's house.

"Communism has made the people harder, even bitter. It's difficult to know who to trust. Double-crossing has become a way of surviving. Everyone for himself."

Anca hoped Evdochia wasn't predicting what might happen in the next days. She studied Evdochia's face as she broke some more twigs for the fire. There was something about her dark eyes that still mesmerized Anca. They were black like coal, but warm and shining bright.

Evdochia returned to the table and sipped another cup of tea, waiting for Anca to talk first.

"Why do I feel that the years seem like weeks?" Anca asked. "It feels like nineteen weeks since I was here."

"Yes," Evdochia agreed. "Our souls don't age. Neither does the heart. If you are good."

"What is good?"

"How can you ask me that? You're the educated one."

"As a doctor, I only know what's bad and should be eliminated." Anca walked away from the fire.

Evdochia poured some more tea. "When someone makes you laugh or something makes you cry, stop a moment. You have found what is true. What is true is good."

"I've missed you."

"Fate has brought us together to do something good."

Anca walked around the room and picked up a photo of Evdochia's son. "Tanase is a kind boy."

The mother smiled. "I tried. He's all I have."

"He's a year older than my daughter, Sandra. When I left our town, I was pregnant."

Evdochia stood up and put a log on the fire. She didn't comment. Anca explained, "Petre chose his work."

"Like Tanase's father. He also had work he wanted to do, but there was no work in Romania for Gypsies. So he left. Went to Germany." She looked down.

Anca thought of her friends, the Four Musketeers. *We are the poets of our lives.* Strong women. Evdochia also. "Was it your choice not to marry another man?"

"Yes. I was hurt. And you?"

"Me, too. I had my child's love, and it was enough."

"Do you think we were wrong?"

"We made the choices we wanted. I'm sure you could have married many men."

Evdochia smiled. "Several men wanted me, but I had my work…" She hesitated, and then winked at Anca with her secret. "I was busy taking care of Tanase. I felt full inside."

Anca understood, and then she asked, "What do you think is more important for a woman? To be a better mother or better wife?"

"Can't you be both?"

"Yes, of course—but it may be hard to do both very well at the same time."

Evdochia shrugged. "There are more mothers than wives."

"Yes."

"Women who are wives may live with their husbands for a longer time than they do with their children. So maybe the answer has something to do with the number of years."

Anca wasn't sure. "Once you're a mother, you're always a mother," Anca said, "even if your child doesn't live with you anymore. You always act like a mother, whether they're small or grown up or far away. While if you stop being a wife, you stop being a wife."

"You can be both," Evdochia insisted. "A woman does what she does best: she holds things together, whether it's her man or her child or her world." She shrugged. "You're here, after all these years. Maybe that's because you want an answer to your question."

"How did you know?"

"I'm a Gypsy."

They both laughed.

"Don't tell me you read my palm without my realizing it?" Anca teased her.

"Only your right one, the one that counts."

Anca looked at her right palm and then the left. "Is there a difference?"

"Of course, and your returning to Romania shows the difference. Let's go over our plans for tomorrow. Petre may not be completely satisfied by the outcome of the revolution, but he did achieve his goal. Now he should leave before they kill him."

Petre's situation crystallized in Anca's mind. It's all real now: he's trying to escape. It's a race against time.

"I noticed as I drove out of Bucharest there are tanks moving into the capital," Anca said.

The Gypsy nodded. "The KGB wants to keep Ileyesco in power, and the CIA opposes him. In addition, they don't want Petre killed by the Russians or the Romanians. Petre may have to regroup from abroad."

Anca listened and then pressed her friend back to their mission. "How should we arrange the escape?"

"This is what we'll do…"

—————

After dinner, Anca and Evdochia prepared the wagon. "There's fresh straw in the basement. Let's get it."

They made several trips until Evdochia was satisfied with the wagon's external appearance. "I'll show you how the trap door works in the wagon."

Then they walked behind the hut. "The night is clear," remarked Anca. She examined the stars, hoping to assess the next day's weather. "Maybe we should leave an hour earlier and go directly to the Hungarian border."

Evdochia shook her head no. "I don't want to change my regular schedule. It could look suspicious. In addition, I've received word from WDC that Petre is alive and safe. He left Mokess and his family in Vinga, a small town midway between Timisoara and Arad. After the first night of cross-country skiing, Mokess's wife, Edit, became weak. Mokess stayed behind while Petre and the priest continued together to another convent nearer the Hungarian border. Petre is aware that a Gypsy and nun will take him across the border. He will trust us."

Anca nodded. Evdochia was firmly in charge.

"Look, Anca, this is the handle for the trap door." Evdochia showed Anca the stick Tanase had made to raise the slab of wood. "The false bottom is under the driver's seat. It's made so the seat looks like it has steps from the outside, but inside it's hollow."

"Is it large enough?" Anca examined the hiding place. "Petre is six foot one."

"Tanase got into it yesterday. He's as tall as Petre. He stayed on his back and bent his knees up to his chest."

"You'll have to drive the horses slowly once Petre's in."

"I've been doing this route forever with fragile eggs." Evdochia bellowed her hearty laugh. "My schedule is like clockwork. I'm at each convent at exactly the same time. At the Hungarian border, there are the same guards every day. That's why it's important we don't change my schedule. I know only those who guard the border at the time when I'm there."

Anca nodded. "I understand." Anca knew that she had to be patient, but the anticipation of seeing Petre was filling her with fear. She kept taking deep breaths to calm the pounding of her heart.

"We'll pick up the eggs tomorrow morning at five o'clock. It'll take thirty minutes to load the wagon."

"Do you have my disguise?" asked Anca.

"Yes, and a veil, too. Petre shouldn't see your face or recognize you at all."

24

TRANSYLVANIA, ROMANIA

December 28,1989

> *Come then, put away your sword in its sheath, and let us two go lay together in the bed of love, so that we may have faith and trust in each other.*

— HOMER, *THE ODYSSEY*, BOOK 10

TWO WOMEN WERE PERCHED on top of an old-fashioned wagon traveling toward the rising sun. They sat erect as they moved through the snow. The darker one, dressed in a black Gypsy coat and black fur hat, held the horses' reins. The taller one, dressed in a black nun's robe and black veil, held on to a basket of eggs. Below their feet, but behind them, were dozens of egg boxes that were spread out carefully in straw.

Anca sat quietly, looking around and admiring the beginning of day. No one else was on the road. It could have been any small European town or country. She wondered what Greece looked like, or Ithaca. How had Penelope felt when she saw Odysseus after twenty years? Athena and the goddesses had made her beautiful for her man.

"We'll continue south from Arad to Sagu," said the Gypsy, interrupting Anca's thoughts. "Then ten more miles to Vinga, our second convent." Evdochia knew the road by heart. She knew where it turned and where it stopped. She knew when to change the horses' pace and when to shift her weight.

"Who told you Reverend Mokess stayed at Vinga?" Anca asked, focusing on assessing the network.

"Steven, WDC from the State Department. He has been working with Petre long before he helped you in Vienna."

Anca wasn't surprised. "Does Petre know I'm here?" She swallowed her words. The thought of seeing him was making her stomach queasy.

"No, for sure not." Evdochia sensed Anca's agitation next to her. "I asked Steven the same question."

"What did he say?"

Evdochia didn't answer; she had been trained to never say more than she should. Even when questioned, she omitted half the information she had. Communism and the CIA had formed her well.

"He said that Petre had parted ways from Father Strancusi because they were being followed."

"Is someone after Petre?"

"Possibly... maybe one of Ceausescu's terrorists, Iranian or Libyan, or a Romanian communist or even a Russian KGB agent. Petre's head would be a big prize."

Anca heard her stomach rumble, but she wasn't hungry. "Does Steven know where Petre is?"

"He said he's in one of the convents near the Hungarian border, waiting to cross over. Petre knows we're delivering eggs to the convent and we'll take him to safety in a wagon."

Evdochia felt Anca's fears and tried to comfort her. "We'll ask in the next town. The mother superior, Sister Julia Rosu, is a friend."

Anca remembered that the word *friend* took on another dimension in Romania. It meant protection and loyalty. Often, it meant life.

"The convent is off the road, toward the second silo on the left."

Anca turned her head, but all she could see were snow-covered hills and fields. She kept wondering what her first words to Petre would be. How would she act? How would he act? Would he be happy to see her?

"Are you hungry?" Evdochia asked.

"No, not at all."

"If you change your mind, I packed some cheese and fruit. We can stop to eat."

"Let's go on. We're almost there."

"As we turn, you'll see an old iron gate. There's a terrible man who's in charge of it."

Evdochia rode up to the gate, got off the wagon, and pulled the bell's rope. She climbed back up, redraped the blanket over their legs, and waited.

An old man hobbled toward them. "Don't make so much noise!" he yelled.

Anca and Evdochia watched the figure move closer and then open the gate. He was dressed in tattered clothes, no overcoat, no hat, and no shoes, despite the snow and cold. His feet were bare and cut. Frozen mud and pus were embedded in his toes.

Evdochia slapped the horses with the reins to move faster. "I don't want them to stop in front of him. He's a devil."

Anca looked at the wobbly figure. At first she only saw an old, bent man trying to walk in the snow. His body looked as worn out as his clothes. He grumbled and cursed as he limped barefoot to avoid the ice. Then he spat at a tree.

"Who is he?" she asked.

"Siminescu. He's *bad*." Evdochia muttered the word *bad* with all her Gypsy soul. "During the war, he was the leader of Romania's Iron Guard, whose goal was to kill Jews. Their headquarters were in Bucharest and it became a torture center for kidnapped Jews. They set up an archery field with crossbows in the courtyard and stripped each Jew naked. Then they aimed arrows at their genitals."

"Oh, my God," Anca gasped. She felt a shiver go through her body.

Suddenly, the horses surged in their traces. "Whoa!" shouted Evdochia as the horses tried to gallop away in fright.

"Give me one second to stop here," Evdochia said. She went to check the eggs. Satisfied they were intact, she then patted the horses to calm them. "He's gone. It's all right."

Turning to Anca, she said, "We'll give these eggs to the mother superior and see if she needs any more for visitors. She'll give us a hint about Petre."

Anca jumped off the wooden seat, all the time holding on to her nun's robe. She wasn't comfortable in her role.

"*Buna dimineata*," greeted the Mother superior, her round face beaming. "Is this your friend from Moldova that Tanase said is visiting?"

"*Da*, she doesn't speak. She's mute. We communicate in sign language."

Anca realized Evdochia didn't want her to talk in any language. Probably afraid that Anca would be nervous and make a mistake.

The nun smiled softly at the women. Then she walked toward the door to close it. "Sit down and join me for tea," she offered, taking the basket of eggs from Evdochia.

"Thank you," smiled the Gypsy to her friend and asked, "Do you need more eggs *today*?"

"No, not *today*. *Yesterday*."

Anca closed her eyes. Thank God. She wasn't ready yet to see Petre.

"Oh, that's too bad," responded Evdochia. "Do you know where they may need more eggs *today?*"

The mother superior passed them a tray of warm cakes and rose petal jam. "Maybe at Semiac, yes, nearer to the Hungarian border by now."

Someone knocked at the door. A nun walked in without waiting for the mother superior's word, "Enter." She eyed Anca suspiciously as if she could smell her fear. She stared at the Gypsy long and hard.

Evdochia stood up. "Thank you very much for tea. I must continue my deliveries. Until tomorrow."

They left quickly without looking back.

Anca and Evdochia rode for an hour speaking little. Anca kept looking behind them to see if they were being followed. She was also preoccupied, thinking about what she'd say to Petre when she'd see him.

"We're nearing Semiac," the Gypsy said. "The Mures River runs through town. That's why we're feeling a cool breeze. Soon we'll see fog." At that moment, a thick gray fog descended, enveloping the women and covering the road before them in a mysterious cloak of beauty.

"How did you know we'd drive into fog?"

"I smelled it."

Anca tried to smell it. She sniffed—nothing.

"Maybe you can smell if there's a doctor in town named Petre," Anca said, half-jokingly.

Evdochia breathed in again and calmly answered, "I smell the cologne of pine trees."

Anca gasped. Pine trees. Evdochia's telephone message in New York was, *"Pine trees are in trouble."*

Anca almost fell off the wagon. "You guessed."

"I guessed what?" Evdochia was surprised.

"When I first met Petre, he was wearing a cologne that smelled of pine. My daughter says he still wears it." Anca couldn't believe Evdochia had actually smelled Petre's cologne from such a distance, or even that her phone message had predicted Petre's situation.

"If it makes you happy to think I guessed it, I guessed it."

Anca stared at the Gypsy. *What was true? Did Evdochia really have visionary powers?*

Anca remained silent, trying to figure out what the Gypsy's prediction meant. She wondered if Evdochia was aware that Petre had been in danger three weeks ago. Perhaps she knew that her phone call would summon Anca to help Petre, even before he escaped.

Then she thought, *What will happen if Petre doesn't find me attractive? What if he doesn't have any interest in me?* She thought for a moment that he and the CIA might just be using her to accomplish this escape. She fidgeted insecurely in her disguise.

Hearing a noise, she turned her head. "Probably an animal," she said, trying to calm herself. "What do we do if someone is following us?"

The Gypsy didn't answer. Instead she stated, "The building on the right is the convent."

"We're here already?"

Evdochia pulled the reins in. "Let's go," and she put two boxes of eggs into the straw basket.

"Wait—I'm not ready." Anca tried to comb her short black hair with her fingers and redden her cheeks with a few pinches. She couldn't do much under the circumstances. She thought of Athena and how lucky Penelope was.

"Put the veil on tightly," Evdochia reminded her. "Don't let anything more than your eyes show." Then she added, "Pine trees are here," and she pointed to her nose.

Anca tried to jump off the seat, but her robe got caught on the wooden stick. She tripped and fell down.

"Let me help you," offered the Gypsy and gave her a hand.

"I'm so nervous."

"Walk next to me, not behind me. Remember, don't reveal yourself."

The two women in black, one with the rough clothes of life and the other with the soft threads of faith, walked side by side.

"Good afternoon," said the mother superior to Evdochia.

"This is my friend from Moldova," responded the Gypsy. "She's mute, so don't be offended if she doesn't answer your questions."

Anca nodded. The nun answered with a bow.

"This must be the season for visiting friends," began the heavyset nun. "I have a visitor also. Yesterday I had two, but one left during the night."

Anca sat down on the wooden bench in the corner of the sparsely furnished room.

Evdochia gave Anca a wink. "Yes, I thought you might need some more eggs."

"I do." The mother superior's voice rang like a cash register. "How should we arrange payment for a *golden egg?*"

Anca fidgeted in her seat. She wanted to remind Evdochia that she had a lot of dollars with her, but she was supposed to be mute.

Evdochia said, "How much do you think an extra egg is worth?"

"If it's truly golden, I should quote you in gold. Romanian money is worth nothing. American dollars will do."

"That's fair," Evdochia responded, and began bargaining. "I have five thousand dollars to donate so that you can redo your roof."

The nun smiled. "How kind of you to think of protecting us

from the snow. Our sanctuary also needs a stove. Eight thousand dollars will keep us well-nourished so we'll have the strength to pray." She crossed herself and smiled.

"How about six thousand dollars?" Evdochia offered.

The nun looked at Anca, bowed to her, and gave her final bid. "Seven thousand dollars. Certainly your treasure is worth that."

Anca nodded. Evdochia took the cue and asked the mother superior to give them a minute alone. The nun left.

Anca took out seven piles of one-hundred-dollar bills. Steven had given her ten packs when he visited her in the U.S. Mission. Each pack contained a thousand dollars.

Anca was sweating, and her hands shook as she raised her robe and counted the wads of dollar bills. She gave seven piles to Evdochia, who put the money inside the straw basket of eggs. Then she called the nun back into the room and passed her the basket.

"With God's blessings," said the Gypsy. "Please lead your visitor to the courtyard. Is anyone there?"

"No."

"Good. I'll lead the horses to the well." Evdochia stopped and thought. "After you come with your guest, give us ten minutes alone to rearrange my wagon. Remember, no one can be near us for ten minutes."

"Don't you trust us here?"

"Only if you give me your word before God that no one will follow us after we leave."

"It is done," and the nun crossed herself as she looked at the crucifix next to the safe where she had just put her money.

As planned, Evdochia and Anca led the horses to the courtyard. Anca indicated with her hands that Evdochia should lead the visitor to the wagon and help him into the hiding place. Anca touched her heart and made a grimace indicating that she was too nervous to help. Then she walked over to a dark corner so as to look at Petre without his knowing she was there.

Anca waited. She listened. She tried to calm herself by taking deep breaths. As she was breathing deeply, she heard the sound of footsteps. She felt faint. She leaned against the stone wall.

Petre emerged from the doorway. She saw his silhouette, tall and straight. His shoulders were broader than she remembered and his arms seemed stronger, but he also looked thinner. A week-old stubble hid his chin and shadowed his skin. She studied the changed face and how the years had lined his cheeks. There was a vertical line that divided his forehead in half. The lips she had dreamed of kissing night after night kissing her were tighter now; they turned downward. Unexpectedly, a burst of light bathed the courtyard and she saw his blue eyes sparkle the same way she remembered, deep, furtive, and penetrating. They were as intense as the passion she felt watching him.

She retreated toward a corner away from the ray of light so as not to be noticed. She waited, breathing deeply as he ran toward the wagon. She wanted to join him, but her legs wouldn't move. She willed her body to push forward, but she was chained by fear. She felt as if her chest had been nailed to the wall. Her legs stiffened, they felt heavy. She wanted to run towards him, but she was barely able to walk. Then her courage returned slowly and willed her legs to gather strength.

She put her hand over the veil to hide her face. She covered her mouth with the curtain of silk; only her eyes could speak the truth. She approached the wagon, nodded at Evdochia and gave a quick look at Petre. She intended just a passing gaze, as a way of announcing her presence, but her eyes lingered on his. Feelings took over without her control. Her body language expressed them all.

Petre met the nun's green eyes and wondered what they were telling him. They reminded him of a rainy night in the country-side. The time between seasons, with red and yellow leaves falling on the green grass. He wanted to caress this woman. He wanted to bury his lips against the worried brow, wipe away the lines of time. He couldn't look away.

The woman's eyes were drilling a hole into him. His heart was being pried open by her softness, stinging him with her desire to help. Who was this woman behind the veil? What was her warm stare telling him? Distracted by the need to escape, he couldn't look more.

The Gypsy lowered her head so Petre wouldn't recognize her and led him into the wagon's hiding place. She helped him into the hollowed opening and showed him how to raise his knees while she lowered the cover. On top of his secret place, she spread out the hay and boxes of eggs.

Anca cleared a seat for herself on top of the slab of wood. She moved her veil slightly to the side to better see what was in front of her. The silk caught her earrings.

Petre lay in the dark. His back bumped against the false door as the horses began to walk. He kept thinking of the veiled eyes, expressing... what? Hurt?

Then he recalled that light had touched the earrings–green— his mother's earrings. Anca's eyes. The earrings and eyes were the same vibrating waves of green sea from his dreams.

He remembered the day in the countryside when he'd hid behind a tree to have one last look before she left. He had held on tightly to the tree's trunk, digging his nails into its bark as if he were digging into his own skin, punishing himself for letting her go. He had held on so tightly that the bark peeled off leaving it bare to winters of neglect.

He tried to breathe deeply in his small hiding space, but he couldn't; he was stifled. He looked at the plank of wood above him.

Only two slits were visible and little air or light passed through. The wagon moved over rocks and chunks of icy mud, and his legs hit the hard wood. The gnawing sensation in his stomach persisted. It felt like a hollow hole being filled with pain.

"Anca, Anca," he whispered. He wet his dry lips and tried to speak her name. "Anca." He tried to lean toward her side and feel the warmth from her robe. Instead, he swayed back and forth in his tight hole. He raised his hands to the wood above and tried to touch her body. He breathed in deeply and tried to sense her near.

"Anca, what are you doing here?"

In all his dreams, he had never thought she would return to him.

Crouched in the dark shelter, he couldn't reach out to her. He couldn't tell her how sorry he was that he had let her go. He had never forgiven himself. He had wanted to protect her, save her, give to her, but he hadn't. He wanted to hold up the revolution to her like a knight proving his love, but he had to abdicate. He wanted to show her that he had fought to end communism so he could be free to return to her. He wanted so much to be her hero, to give her his glory. Instead, she had come to save him, to pull him out of the dark depths of Hell.

He blamed himself for nineteen years lost, the passion of youth wasted, and time gone forever. He knew that he had let ambition get in his way, that it was his fault that their love had not been shared.

———

"How much longer?" Anca asked Evdochia.

"Another ten minutes to the border. We'll see a lot of guards on the Romanian side and after three hundred meters, we'll see just as many on the Hungarian side. Tighten your veil. We're coming to the first patrol. Remember, don't talk."

Anca's heart was beating hard. Had Petre recognized her? When he stared at her and their eyes met, she felt his hurt. She felt he had wanted to say so much.

"Good evening, Evdochia," greeted a young soldier. "Saw your son yesterday. He said you'd give me some eggs today."

"Take some." She smiled. "Send my best to your wife."

"Thanks a lot," he said, lifting out several eggs. Then he flagged her on.

Evdochia nodded hello over and over to the file of Romanian guards. To them, she was delivering her eggs, just as on any other morning.

"*Jonapot kivanok.* Hello," said the first of the Hungarian guards at the border.

"*Jonapot kivanok,*" repeated Evdochia.

"Are you sure you're not a Hungarian Gypsy? You speak like a native."

"*Igen.* Yes," she said and they both laughed. "Give me your palm," Evdochia said in Hungarian. "I'll read your future."

"Just my future for tonight. I have a date with a blonde beauty."

"Yes, I see your future, and yes, she is willing," smiled Evdochia and pointed to his love line. "Here are some eggs—for strength."

"Go on, pass, Evdochia," he said chuckling and slapped the horse's flank.

"You know, I still read coffee grounds," Evdochia whispered to Anca as they continued on.

"I'm not surprised."

"Last month I was having a séance with a young woman. She asked me to read her fortune from the leftover coffee at the bottom of her cup. When I looked, I saw nothing."

"Why?"

"Because there was no future. The next week a rabid dog bit her. She died."

Anca shuddered, thinking of her own future, and the next step of their escape. Would they be pursued? What would be the future for her and Petre?

———

Evdochia continued driving through the border patrol, waving to some guards, greeting others, stopping to give out eggs along the way.

"Five more minutes," Evdochia whispered to Anca. "Then we'll be at the train station."

Anca tried to count the minutes away, but she couldn't concentrate. Instead, she counted the number of guards as the horses trotted and the number of eggs the Gypsy gave for good will.

"The train station is behind the last convent," Evdochia explained. "That's when you and Petre will get out of the wagon." She looked up at the sky. "The sun will set in ten minutes."

"When's our train?"

"In seven minutes. It's the train that goes west. Two minutes before the train arrives, there's a change of guards at the border. Usually, within this time there's a lot of commotion because the guards know each other and spend time chatting, especially now. The revolution has given them a lot to talk about."

Anca looked around, assessed the setting sun and the stationmaster's hut.

"We'll have to be quick," Evdochia warned. "As soon as the train stops, I'll lead you and Petre to the platform's staircase. Move inside quickly. Buy the tickets in the train. Do you have the passports?"

Anca touched her bag under her robe. "Listen, Evdochia, I'm going to say goodbye now, fast." Anca felt like she was going to cry.

The Gypsy led her carriage to the rear of the train station. She dropped the horses' reins and let her hands free. Anca took them in hers. It seemed that only yesterday she had admired the Gypsy's scarred hands as they placed twigs and sticks into the fire without feeling pain. Somehow, they appeared even stronger today.

"Forget me not," Evdochia said.

"I shall never forget you and I'll never forget what you've done for me." Anca smiled, "Before we part—I left my suitcase and bags in your house. There's an envelope in the zippered part. Everything is for you. My address is there, too. Write me."

Evdochia nodded, then she caressed Anca's veil and black robe. "God sent you."

The train whistled. Anca jumped off the seat and tapped on the false door. Both women, as one, lifted the slab of wood and helped Petre stand up.

He took Evdochia's hand and then smiled, recognizing her. Anca placed her cheek next to her friend's. Evdochia leaned against her wagon so as not to cry.

"Go—now!"

PART V

TOGETHER

DECEMBER 28-29, 1989

The Wedding of Penelope and Odysseus

25

HUNGARY AND PARIS

December 28-29,1989

> *Now from his breast into the eyes that ache of longing*
> *mounted, and he wept at last, his dear wife, in his arms....*
> *And so, she too rejoiced, her gaze upon her husband, her*
> *arms around him pressed as though forever.*

— HOMER, *THE ODYSSEY*, BOOK 23

THE TRAIN TRAVELED WESTWARD. Anca and Petre sat nervously in their compartment, silent, listening for any sign that they were being followed. He stood up every minute to look out the window, his face hidden beneath the narrow curtain. She watched him. Under his right eye a muscle twitched. He'd sit down and then stand up, making furtive movements with his lips without saying a word.

She wondered who would speak first. Their eyes met; hers spoke of hurt, his of sorrow. She moved closer to him.

"Hold me."

Their arms pressed around each other tightly. Bound by emotions stronger than words, there they stayed, hardly breathing, afraid to awaken from their dream.

Petre took Anca's hand to his lips and softly kissed each finger. She put her head in his lap and she wept, feeling his lips against her cheeks.

"Please forgive me," he said, taking her in his arms. "I'm so sorry."

His fingers opened her veil and he caressed the fine lines surrounding her eyes. "It was hard for you alone."

What should she answer—should she blame him for lying to her? She had lived so many years without him. She closed her eyes.

"I was selfish. I only thought of my dreams, my work. I left you with nothing."

"You gave me our daughter."

Petre wiped the tears from his cheeks. "I'll make it up to you. I promise."

"Where do you want to go?" she asked, attempting to change the subject and lighten their mood.

"Is this a magic train?"

She smiled into his eyes. "Make a wish. Anywhere in Europe and we'll stop there."

"Paris. I've always wanted to walk with you in Paris."

"*Quelle coïncidence.* This train goes west. Vienna first, then Paris. Are you up to seeing friends?"

"Not yet. Just you." He put his head against her breast and wrapped his arms around her waist. She felt his anguish.

"Petre," she whispered in his ear. "I'm supposed to be a nun. What happens if the conductor walks in?"

He jumped, nervous, looked to the door, his gaze intense. He stood up and stared out the window. He sat down next to her, rigid, considering multiple scenarios of imminent danger and what could happen next.

Anca caressed his stubbly chin. "Let me first give you these papers and explain." She hoped his need to focus on tangible matters would calm his thoughts. She began: "I had a visitor the other day at the U.S. Mission, Steven Bradley. He gave me a passport for you and some information…"

After the exchange of papers and micro-discs, Anca looked into the world of Petre's blue eyes, feeling an electric response to his body as if she were waking up from a long sleep.

"I want to know everything about you," he whispered. "What you've done all these years. What you think. Where you go. Who you see," and he paused and looked down. "Who…"

"You're asking too many questions." She wasn't ready to open herself for fear she'd begin with expressing her resentment. She certainly didn't want to tell him about Mark right now.

Petre brought her close to him and pressed her hard to his chest.

She inched away. "I keep thinking the conductor will walk in without knocking on the door."

He snapped off her veil and kissed her to silence. Their lips met with all the passion of remembering and wanting. He couldn't stop kissing her and hugging her.

"Have I changed a lot?" the woman in her murmured.

"You're more beautiful than ever. When I look at you I still see the shy girl who tripped on the steps of the clinic."

"Well, I'm not shy anymore." Her initial fear of being alone with him had passed. She wanted to rejoice and be happy that they had found each other. She kept kissing him, rubbing her cheek next to his, and feeling the bristles from his beard to be sure he's real.

"Yes, you are strong and shy. That's your charm."

"I think you look more handsome now. Stronger, more muscular, though thinner. Mysterious too, your furrowed brow, especially your smile. An enigma."

Petre didn't respond. He tried to relax, breathing in deeper, trying to calm himself. Anca watched, concerned.

"You'll have to give me time," he said, moving slightly away from her. "I've been through a lot. I never expected to see you again. I can't believe you're here." He stood up, paced the small compartment.

She remembered hearing about soldiers in shock, returning from war. The trauma lingers. It takes time.

"More than twenty years, and they threw me out. I did it all. Toppled Ceausescu, dismantled the training ground, and the nuclear institute. I led them to victory." He slammed his fist several times on the wall. "Without me, none of it would have been achieved!"

Anca listened. Ambition had crept into his motivation, and so his disappointment was that much deeper. She knew she'd have to be patient with him.

"I can't believe you did this for me," he whispered, moving to her, taking her in his arms, becoming softer, more tender. "Is it possible you can forgive me? Will you trust me?" He pressed his lips against her neck.

She pulled away, feeling confused. Loving him and yet still hurt.

He moved back. "Yes, let's talk. Sandi told me over the years about your beginnings in New York. I had to learn from her about you. I know my friends in Vienna helped you get started in a New York hospital, but tell me, how did you manage after that?"

She hesitated, wanting to control her anger, to choose her words. "I had to start from the beginning with an internship program in pediatrics, then residency, exams, and so on. It was hard."

She didn't tell him that she'd had to take the specialty and program his friends had found for her, or that she'd chosen the simplest type of general pediatrics rather than specializing because anything else would have taken more years. It was easier to stay full time in the hospital than to build a private practice. She told him about Mica and André helping her start at New York Hospital. She didn't say anything about Mark easing her life. She wasn't ready to tell him that. Yet she knew Petre was aware there had been another man in her life. Sandra had told him. Mica, Cristina, Marina, and Alec—they had all told him.

It would be hard for Petre to hear it from her. She decided she'd wait for the right moment.

"I have wronged you and made your life harder rather than easier," he said. "Please don't hold it against me forever. You must forgive me."

Tears rolled down her cheeks. For so many years, she had dreamed of hearing his remorse, his apology, and now, it hurt too much. She knew she needed time also to forgive.

"Tell me about Sandi," he said. "How did you arrange to work and take care of her at the same time?"

He moved closer to Anca and refocused his thoughts away from himself to concentrate on her. He saw how her voice softened when she spoke of Sandi, hardened when she spoke of medicine.

"Work was my anchor and escape."

She moved away from him. "I've been talking too much. I must stop." She started to breathe deeply like him. Was his nervousness contagious? Or was it her nervousness that was contagious to him? "Tell me about you," she said.

"Where should I begin?" He thought of the last few weeks. He had become an animal, a beast, plotting, killing, running away. He heard pounding in his head, guns blasting, people crying, dying. He had been in the middle of it all.

"I'm out of power. It will take me time to get used to that. I'm no longer needed."

She stood up, took his hand, and put it to her lips.

He freed himself, and paced up and down. "I'm not the same man. Have you thought about what we'll do? Stay together? You knew about this before I did." He stopped, realizing his words sounded like a reproach. "Anca, let's not part again."

She took a deep breath, wanting to trust him. "Don't say that until you're sure. I don't want you to feel obligated just because I'm helping you escape. If you feel indebted to me, I will leave now."

"What are you talking about? I love you. I always did. Always will."

"*Shh, shh,*" she murmured as she stroked his silky blond hair.

A conductor knocked on the door. Petre jumped, and Anca moved away from him.

"Thank God there's a curtain on the door," she said. "A nun and a man."

"He didn't see us. Do you have tickets?"

"No, I'll buy them from him. Let's speak in English, confuse him. We can't trust him."

"*Joestet kivanok.* Good evening," said the Hungarian conductor as he entered their compartment. He spoke in Hungarian, saying, "Can I please have your passports? Also your tickets and documents. Your identification papers."

"Good evening." Anca tried to use a crisp British accent and appear calm.

"No speak English," he responded. "Do you speak Hungarian? *Vorbiti romaneste?* Speak Romanian?"

"No, I'm sorry. Only English," she insisted.

The conductor pointed to Petre.

"No, only English," repeated Anca in the same clipped manner as before. She didn't want Petre to speak, since his English was more accented than hers.

The conductor shook his head several times. Anca saw his shrewd eyes go to Petre's frayed clothes, his drawn-out look, the dirty beginning of a beard, his shabby appearance like a beggar.

"Passport." The conductor persisted and inched his hand closer to Anca's robe.

She slapped the passports in his hand.

"Americans?" He stared again at Petre. Reluctantly, he returned the blue passports.

"Tickets," he said in an annoyed voice.

Anca took out three one-hundred-dollar bills. In an even crisper English, cutting her words so he could never understand her, she said, "We were too late to buy tickets. Here. Dollars. For tickets."

The conductor took the bills, snapped them, pulled them to test the paper's strength. He took out his flashlight and turned the bills over and over in the light.

"Where to?" he said, pointing out the window. "Vienna?"

"Paris." Anca raised two fingers, pointing to herself and then to Petre.

The conductor smirked at her. Raising three fingers, he said in perfect English, "Three more of these hundred-dollar bills if you want *two tickets* to Paris?"

Anca mumbled something, then fumbled in her pocket, and handed him another three bills. He repeated the same ritual, even smelling the money.

"*Koszonom.* Thank you." He smiled and handed her two tickets. "Have a good trip," he said again in perfect British English, and put the crisp green bills in his pocket as he closed the door behind him.

Petre laughed. "You haven't forgotten your Hungarian." He

imitated the conductor, weaseling his hand in front of her robe. *"Jegyeket,* tickets," and wiggled his fingers more.

She pulled his pinky. It felt good to lighten their mood.

"Yeow! I'll get you." He pretended to pull each finger on her hand, and as she cried *yeow,* he kissed her.

"Shh," she whispered. "Our friend will come back and want more dollars."

Petre stopped playing. His face changed expression. The nerve under his eye pulsated. "You have a lot of hundred-dollar bills. Where did you get them?"

"From Steven." She showed him a wad of bills. "This is what was left over from what I paid the mother superior for her golden egg—and this pile of hundreds belongs to you."

She waved a very heavy pack in the air. "It's a fraction of the money you gave Sandra over the years to give to me. I have much more for you in New York."

"Didn't you use it?" he asked surprised. "What about Sandi's schooling?"

"She was an honor student, so she went to good public schools. Gave me time to save for college. And then she got a scholarship."

He looked down, ashamed. "What about paying the rent? Food?"

"I received a good salary from the hospital. I had enough, so I deposited the payments from the CIA in an account for you."

In that instant, Anca realized she had never given up hope that she would find him again. "Petre, I saved it for you, for now. You're a rich man." Her face changed expression and laughter brightened her cheeks. She was happy. She was right not to have given up hope. "Now you know the truth. I want you for your money."

"Well, if you want me only for my money, you can have it all," he said, pretending to throw his money away. *"Garçon. Champagne."*

"Petre, if you don't give me all the champagne I want, I won't tell you how much money you have."

"Garçon. Vite alors. Encore du champagne."

She pretended to raise her glass to him. *"Noroc.* To life. *A nous."*

As they pretended to toast each other, they realized their silliness was only an excuse to stop thinking that they could be caught at any moment. The conductor could return, bringing someone else. Prison. Torture. Life finished—this time forever.

Petre closed his eyes and said he was tired. Would she mind if he took a short nap?

"What a good idea," she said, understanding he had traveled by night and slept by day for the past week. "My lap will be your pillow, and I'll have the pleasure of holding you."

He kissed her and placed himself at her side. Within a minute, he had fallen asleep with his head resting on her thighs. She listened to him breathing. The vertical line on his forehead pulsated, and she felt her heart throb as she watched him sleep.

She closed her eyes and breathed with him in the same rhythm. As the train continued its journey, she leaned her shoulder closer to the window and watched the hills and mountains pass by. She was leaving her country for a second time. Putting her eyes closer to the glass, she imagined the windowpane was a kaleidoscope and she was watching the colors of her country pass by. The red sun began to set, coloring the snow on the mountains in shades of crimson. The sky appeared to be splintering into a thousand fires. No painter could have brushed red so passionately on white and blue.

With each kilometer the train traveled, life in Eastern Europe moved farther and farther away. She stared through the small opening and watched scenes of blue rivers and rushing brooks, green pine trees in between mountain cliffs, a white and blue waterfall. She tried to hear the silence of the hills. The sounds were softer than she had remembered.

It all seemed unreal. Within several days she had found Petre and her life had changed. Now watching him sleep and listening to him breathe, she felt she was right to have returned to Romania to help him. She remembered all she had learned from being a doctor and how the patients who fought to live *lived*. Now, as she watched Petre sleep, she knew what was important: to love the man in her arms.

She dozed off also, and then awakened when the train slowed down. *We're stopping,* she thought and she froze with fear. *Why are we stopping? Maybe the conductor bragged about his new fortune or called the police.*

Petre moved as he felt the train stop. In a second, the calm of sleep on his face turned dark. His brow furrowed. He left Anca's arms without a word and sat up. Looking out the window he stared in the night and then yelled, *"Wien!"* He read the sign at the station again as if he didn't trust his eyes. "Vienna!" He jumped up and down like a small boy. "Anca, I see St. Stephen's Cathedral. We're in Vienna. I'm free! There's nothing they can do to me now."

He sat down next to her and hid his face. Anca smelled pine trees. The salty water enhanced the perfume of spring. Winter was over.

"Petre, you're a hero. You've done it. A coup d'état. The end of Romania's dictatorship. The reign of terror finished, because of you. We're in Vienna."

He took her in his arms. They were together, free, in Vienna, having escaped, as she wished they had done nineteen years ago.

"Do you know Paris?" Anca asked as the train approached its final destination.

"Yes, I've been here a few times. Meetings and such."

"Do you like it?"

"I used to walk at the edge of the Seine and pretend you were with me. You must have heard me talking to you. Sometimes I could swear you were almost next to me."

Anca smiled with her secret—seeing him at the Seine last spring. She'd tell him tomorrow. She was still ashamed that she had lost him in the fog.

"Imagine if I had met you in Paris by chance?" she said.

"That would have been surreal." He laughed. "Do you come here often?"

"Cristina lives in Paris. I visit her every few months. She's become very successful."

"I know. I saw her recently. She donated a lot of money to buy arms for the revolution. She also made a contact for us with arms dealers through her Israeli textile friends."

Anca remembered Nicky and Florin. "Do you also work with Marina?"

Petre smiled. "Of course. She donated a lot of money for small arms and tanks."

"And Mica?"

"Mica's been at the center–quiet and persistent. Her work with UNICEF and the orphanages in Transylvania has helped our group a lot. She shared her information about Romanian officials who wanted to work with the Americans. Those are the generals who now work with us."

Anca remembered the last time she'd seen Mica at Princeton. She had been apologetic. Probably because she hadn't told Anca she had seen Petre, or that a revolution was imminent and that Petre was at the center. Or that she hadn't told her anything.

"And Alec, my guardian angel? He works with you?"

"Nothing can be done without his contacts. He arranged with some Romanian farmers to get the arms into Timisoara and Transylvania. Without Alec, Marina's money and Mica's contacts wouldn't have helped."

"He admires you."

"I admire him. Does he still look after you?" Petre looked down, ashamed. His mood darkened.

Anca promised herself to be patient. Tactfully, she passed on to another thought. "Did you know that Cristina and Eugen are getting married?"

"They told me. Eugen says his work is finished. Yet he's still concerned about Iran. Once their oil embargo is finished, they'll have billions to invest. I hope wisely. Word is out they'll work with Romania again. It's been a tradition since the Shah."

A cloud crossed Petre's face. "I don't know what the future in Romania will be. The communists are like ghosts–they'll haunt me. They're not ready to give up their investments. Their money. They'll fight us away so they can keep their wealth."

"Think good thoughts," Anca said. "Because of you, the communists are out. You made history."

"Let's not talk about it. I'm not ready. The train's stopping."

"Vive Paris!" she sang, trying to change his mood.

As they left the train station, Petre noticed the large clock. "Do you realize it's midnight?"

"No," she answered. "I don't even know what day it is."

"We're at la Gare Saint-Lazare. It's Friday—sabbath, and I'm rising from my tomb." He remembered how Jesus had told the people to remove the stone for Lazarus. Then Jesus yelled, "Unbind him and let him go."

Suddenly, Petre yelled and laughed, remembering he was free and in Paris. *"I'm with Anca. We're together!"*

Taking her hand, he began to skip with her, and then they danced their way to the Seine, as the twisting river led them to Notre Dame. Petre stopped in front of the cathedral. It reminded him of the church in Bucharest when he was a young boy with his father, and they had gone together to see the Crying Saint.

He remembered how word had spread to the presidential palace. Soldiers in heavy boots had come to inspect; police with rifles came to arrest. They tried to shut the doors, stop the praying. The crowds wouldn't let them. They wanted hope. He and Anca had prayed for the same thing.

He turned to her now. "Can we go inside Notre Dame together?"

The moon was bright, and its colored rays entered the cathedral's stained-glass windows to create a rainbow. She looked above to the gothic arches and admired their height. It was as if they were reaching to heaven. The cut pieces of color resembled a kaleidoscope and crystalized in her memory the vibrant colors of her life with Petre.

She saw the mountains of Transylvania, an autumn evening when pine trees turned gold and the Gypsies gathered grapes. The fiddlers' song–I will love you forever. Music flowed through her as she saw Evdochia's black diamond eyes shining as though through the glass windows. The Gypsy's hands were entering the red fire and yet, she was smiling. The colored glass reminded Anca of nights of love-making with Petre as he rolled her in the bear rug and she whispered, "More, more…"

Anca took Petre's hand and brought it to her lips. Their world together, a kaleidoscope of feelings colored by joy and strife. She saw a blue light pierce through the glass windows, and she knew it meant the promise of a bright day.

Petre led her to a votive candle rack. He took two prayer candles, lit them, and gave one to Anca. Getting on his knees, he prayed, "God forgive me, for I have sinned." She kneeled next to him. He raised his candle to her. "Forgive me."

To forgive? What can be a better proof of love than to forgive?

She looked into his eyes, eyes that reflected the colored lights of the glass windows and she realized her instincts had been right to never stop loving him.

As Anca stared above at the sweeping circular arches, she was reminded of their odyssey of love. A winding road that they had traveled for so long had now taken them to the beginning of their life together. Each one had risked danger to save the other—one using the ruse of a broken tractor, the other using the cover of a horse-drawn wagon. For both, in their loving, had wanted to give the other a safer life. Now they were together to enjoy their love.

He put his arms around her, kissed her, and brought her tight against his chest. They were as one and in the flame of their love.

They were two lovers reunited.

THE END